THE HOUSE OF DAWN

AMERICA READS

Rediscovered Fiction and Nonfiction from Key Periods in American History

THE GREAT DEPRESSION

Little Napoleons and Dummy Directors (1933)
Being the Narrative of the Bank of United States

The Barter Lady (1934)
A Woman Farmer Sees It Through

The House of Dawn (1935)
A Novel

THE HOUSE OF DAWN

BY C. E. SCOGGINS

WESTHOLME
Yardley

Originally published in 1935 by the D. Appleton-Century Company.

Westholme Publishing, LLC
Eight Harvey Avenue
Yardley, Pennsylvania 19067
Visit our Web site at www.westholmepublishing.com

First Printing: September 2009
10 9 8 7 6 5 4 3 2 1

ISBN: 978-1-59416-093-6

Printed in United States of America

THE HOUSE OF DAWN

THE HOUSE OF DAWN

I

RED McDOUGAL lifted his saddle-colored face, his grizzled beard, his sun-bleached eyes across Don Carlos A. Romero's office, and let go a shout that shattered the decorum of that place of books—a bellow such as men had seldom heard from Red McDougal in these later years. Rosa, the prim and pretty secretary, started and dropped her fountain pen. A silk-hatted lawyer, passing in the hall, looked in and frowned. McDougal didn't notice; yet he caught his breath back instantly, sat motionless, as if by immobility he might recall that loud, involuntary cry. Fool, fool, to find a thing like this and make it public!

"*Mira,* Carlos! Look!"

He held his breath. And then he knew that luck at last was with him. Carlos hadn't heard. The scholarly, meticulous director of the National Library of Peru, twice honored by the Royal Academy of Spain, continued calmly to inspect old manuscripts. Carlos was very deaf.

Rosa, obliging, smiled and offered, "*Le llamo?* Shall I call him, Señor McDougal?"

"No!" The word was an explosion. Then McDougal breathed again, and habit came again, the cautious and disarming habit of these later years. He grinned.

"Er—thank you, Rosa. No. It doesn't matter."

Quiet fell again. His thick red fingers trembled a little, clutching the brittle sheets. His eyes tried to go back and read again, make sure he was not mistaken; but he knew he was not mistaken. He had read too carefully before he had dared believe. "City of Lima, City of the Kings—" The stilted forms, the stilted, dull deliberations of a city council dead three hundred years. The faded Spanish script, the ancient spelling—*f*'s for *h*'s, *b*'s for *u*'s, *u*'s for *v*'s—familiar now. Obsolete forms held no obscurity for him, the engineer turned student to forget his own frustration.

What his eye fixed on was a word that was not Spanish. What he saw was not three hundred years ago, only a dozen; yet it stood behind that ancient scene, brought it to sharp reality.

He saw the wide, green, smiling country of the lower Marañon, far to the north from Lima, City of the Kings—beyond the Andes, where the river found a break in the knotted ranges and turned eastward toward the Amazon. He saw a camp behind the Andes, in the country of his dream. Malcolm was there, a slender, sunburned little fellow then, a hardy little sorrel-top, red as his father was before time bleached him to a grizzled roan. Malcolm was there the day the split-nosed Indian sidled from the bush and stood there, staring, caught by curiosity—like any creature of the bush; an Indian like any Indian of the lower Marañon, except for that strange mutilation.

Malcolm had whispered, "Daddy, look! He's got two noses!"

Red McDougal knew the ways of jungle creatures. If you stared straight at them, or made any gesture toward them, they were alarmed; but if you kept on doing something they didn't understand, they might come closer, as a deer creeps toward a fluttering handkerchief. He kept on peering through his transit, making unnecessary gestures to a distant flagman who already held the painted staff square on the cross-hairs of the instrument. Under his breath he murmured to the boy, "Be careful, son. Don't scare him."

And the Indian did come closer. Red McDougal only glanced aside at him, spoke gently, first in the Pana dialect and then the Ucayali: "*Patá asun. Na iqui rag.* Come closer. We are friends."

The man cried, "*Uiracocha! Húxi uiracocha!*"

"*Viracocha.*" That was a title of respect, no more; McDougal was well used to being called Red Lord. Still careful not to turn his full gaze on the man, McDougal asked as calmly as he could, "Where do you come from?"

And the man cried strangely, "*Papa uma iqui*—I am without a father, lord!"

"Come closer." The man came, trembling, and McDougal prompted, "He is dead—your father?"

"Yes, lord! Do not punish him!"

And then McDougal saw the amulet that hung on the bare brown breast—not gold or any precious metal, but a fused and shapeless bit of slag, worn smooth! His own voice shook a little, and he let blue lightning strike those black, fear-widened eyes: "Where did he die?"

And the man answered, choking, "Iscacinga, lord!"

Iscacinga. . . . That was in the days when luck rode always at McDougal's shoulder. Iscacinga—Split-nose, or Two Noses! . . . That was not the mark of any accident. The nose had been split in infancy, neatly divided through the cartilage and bone before it hardened, so that each nostril had a barrel of its own. McDougal tried to soothe the Indian's fear, keep him in camp and question him, but in the night he vanished. Red McDougal left the Marañon, forgot his job, his destiny awhile, and searched behind the Andes; but he found no other man whose nose was split. He found no place called Iscacinga. Indians only answered stupidly, "*Unán timá,* lord. It cannot be known."

But luck was with McDougal still. He found his route across the Andes, feasible at only seven thousand feet; and in the City of the Kings, in those days, the administration had great visions for the future of Peru. A railroad there across the Andes, linking the broad Pacific with the navigable streams that fed the Amazon—linking the seas across Peru! The old Dictator, ruthless and magnificent, could see McDougal's dream—ten years ago, when luck rode always at McDougal's shoulder.

The clock struck twelve. A hand fell on McDougal's

shoulder, not the hand of destiny. Don Carlos A. Romero, frail and dry and courteous, was smiling at him, speaking in the flat voice of the very deaf.

"Well, my Rojillo—little Red One—dost thou mean to lunch today?"

"Er—not now, Carlos. Thanks. I—" Red McDougal's voice, loud for Romero's ears, was husky and uncertain, and his thumb moved hastily to hide a word that seemed to blaze, to leap out of that fading script. Don Carlos didn't notice.

"Hast thou, then, found something of importance?"

"No." McDougal forced himself to meet Romero's mild, inquiring eyes, and managed to speak carelessly: "The council meetings of the early seventeenth century—tedious, thou knowest. But of interest, at least to me."

"To any student of our history. Peru is in your debt, Rojillo."

"Nonsense. I merely pass the time."

Don Carlos nodded, sympathetic. He had known McDougal when McDougal's name was one to conjure with—that massive and dynamic man, assured and hearty, certain of his destiny; McDougal's seat was with the mighty in those days. And he had seen McDougal fade and change, grow hollow and uncertain, clinging to a fading dream. Trying to learn diplomacy, persuasiveness—that mighty man! Typing old manuscripts to pass the time that robbed him of his strength!

Don Carlos asked with sympathetic interest, "How does the typing go?"

McDougal answered listlessly, "Nearly two hundred sheets." Carlos was sorry for him—him, McDougal! Listlessly he tossed aside the sheet he clutched in his thick fingers, let the word show, let Carlos see it if he would. And it no longer blazed. Faded, obscure and meaningless, it merged with a thousand other faded words; it had no more reality. To Carlos, who lived by words, who knew the reach and power of the earth only through words, it brought no vision. And McDougal had no faith. Not really. He knew his luck was gone.

He couldn't stand the pity of that frail, dry, sheltered man. He nodded absently and murmured, "*Buén provecho.* May you enjoy your lunch," and fed a blank sheet into the machine and started typing—punching the keys with heavy, awkward fingers, without speed, but carefully—deciphering, transcribing the dead records of old time.

The quiet deepened in the office of Don Carlos A. Romero, where McDougal sat by sufferance. The modern sound of automobiles in the street diminished; it was noon; Lima, the old City of the Kings, drifted into a restful doze. Feet seldom passed in the tiled corridor. Only the tack, tack, tack of typewriter keys resounded, punched by thick, stubborn fingers—Red McDougal passing the time away, the time that robbed him of his faith, his confidence, his strength.

Then the typewriter screamed. He ripped the sheet

out, crushed it and threw it on the floor, thrust in another sheet and hammered now at speed, not carefully:

DEAR MALCOLM: Never mind looking for a job. Come home. I've found the way to Iscacinga. Do you remember, kid? If you can't raise the money—

II

Malcolm McDougal was no longer news in Panama, but he was still good company. Rufe Hardy and Pete Brennan, of the *Star and Herald,* met him at the boat and asked him, merely as a matter of form, if there was any news about his father's concession in Peru; but what they wanted was to see if they could stick him for the drinks. They tried in Barney's Bar, in the Ajax and in Johnny's Ritz. They tried plain poker dice, *bideux, capitán manda,* Blue Eyes—all the known combinations of five dice. They were still trying in the back room at Rodriguez's, still without much luck, when Pete peered out into the bar and fainted.

A resplendent pair of tourists had just entered. Brennan, having lived ten years in Panama, was sensitive to tourists. Tourists were not people, or at least they didn't act like people—not while they were tourists. Everything they did and said and wore shrieked to the world, "Look, look, we're tourists!"

And this pair were something special. They were tropical beyond belief. The man wore pongee, beautifully tailored, topped by a gleaming helmet such as no old-timer could be bothered with. The girl—she didn't seem quite sure she was a girl. Her double-breasted coat was masculine—daintily masculine. Her creamy Panama, cocked like a man's, had such a flowing sweep as no man's ever dared to have. Seen sidewise, she appeared to wear a skirt, a long slim skirt that just exactly covered her dainty feet yet just exactly didn't touch the floor; but when she cocked her high-heeled slipper on the bar rail—

"Pants," moaned Pete. "Hollywood pants!"

Malcolm McDougal—Mac to everybody but his father—leaned across Pete's plump and stricken form, looked out and grinned.

Rufe Hardy drawled, "You bettah covah up one eye, Mac. Maybe you don't know it, but you're lookin' at a million dollahs."

Malcolm McDougal said, "You're telling me?"

"Uh-huh," said Hardy. "Interviewed him last night. That's J. G. Hall."

"Not what I'm lookin' at," said Mac.

"Oh, that!" said Hardy. "Stick around here, Mac, and you'll get used to anything."

"Not what I'm lookin' at!" said Mac. "You're married; you're not human any more."

Brennan, reviving, muttered, "Gimme air!" and staggered to his feet and bolted through the bar. Passing the objects of his aversion, he said loudly, "On our left, ladees and gemmun, are the Halls of Hollywood!"

The girl turned sharply. Her clear, arrogant young eyes saw three young men, one plump, one thin, one tall and broad and lean, with flaming hair—all hatless and all sunburned in the collegiate manner, so that she forgot that she was in the tropics. Only one of them was looking at her—the tall one, the red-haired one. Her own hair shaded toward mahogany.

She snapped, "Not Hollywood. So what?"

Her escort turned, a still-faced, weary-looking man. He said, "Pay no attention. . . . On your way!"

"So nothing," said the tall one, grinning. "Nothing at all, Miss—Hall, is it? Nobody minds Pete Brennan."

"He's a little drunk," said Rufe, responsible.

"Nobody," moaned Pete.

The escort said more firmly, "That'll do!"

The girl, still looking at the red-haired one, said, "So I see."

He said, "Oh, I'm not Brennan. I'm McDougal."

"I suppose it matters?"

"Well," he grinned, "to me it does."

"And me," said Pete, bitter. "Wha'd'ye think this is—a speak-easy? Wearin' pants and bellyin' up to the bar like a—"

"Shut up," said Rufe Hardy, the responsible. . . . "I'm sorry, Mr. Hall. May I present—"

"I'm goin' back to Boston," said Pete, utterly discouraged.

"—Mr. McDougal, of Peru? I understand—"

"You may not," said the girl, and turned her mannish—girlishly mannish—back.

Rufe Hardy finished manfully, "—he's flying with you to Peru tomorrow."

J. G. Hall said briefly, "That's unfortunate, but I suppose the planes are common carriers."

The girl's voice proved its sex by having the last word. Her eyes fixed in the mirror on the red-haired one, she added, "Very."

But the red one only grinned and turned away. She saw him that night at the railroad station, boarding the open car that was to take them across the isthmus, but he gave no sign of seeing her. There were not many passengers. The lonely lights of the canal were swallowed in the jungle, and black water gleamed in the starlight, sinister, the pitiful bare stumps of forests drowning there; but the young man seemed unaware of any loneliness. He didn't look at her. He didn't look at anything. He only sat there, like a man who rides a street car through familiar streets.

Quite audibly she asked her father, "Isn't that Mr. McDougal?" But the warm wind washed her voice away into the darkness, and the young man didn't seem to hear.

He disappeared in the warm smells and clamor of Colon. He wasn't at the Washington. In the morning, at the airport, in the thick, warm gloom of dawn, she didn't recognize him. He had changed to faded khaki, and he wore a hat—not a white helmet like her father's, not a cool Panama like hers, but a drab, battered felt, as if he didn't know he was in the tropics. Yet he knew his way about. He called the pilot Tom; the pilot called him Mac. At the last moment, when the luggage was all aboard—most of it hers—he crawled down the little hatchway in the roof of the amphibian, crawled into a rearward seat and went to sleep.

The plane roared up in the sudden dawn, wheeled inland across the jungle—in the wrong direction! Or the sun rose in the west. The flat green isthmus, broken with lagoons and lakes, swam underneath; she saw the tiny, broken line of the canal, the town of Panama—it had to be Panama, but it was all twisted and reversed. The red-haired youth slept on. Asleep, he looked queerly older; little muscles hardened about his mouth, in his lean, sunburned cheeks. Her father stared ahead with weary eyes. There were no other passengers.

The plane droned out over open water, into a dull gray fog. The fog pressed hard on the windows. Surely the plane was tilting, wheeling blindly—flying straight down! She cried out to her father, but he couldn't hear. The pilot and the radio operator, in their little cabin, seemed to stare in frozen immobility.

Light stabbed her eyes unbearably; the fog blazed into incandescence all about. The plane swam into sunlight on a vast white sea of cotton. Unimaginably far away, a purple crater opened, rimmed with shadowed cloud cliffs, bottomless. The pilot turned and pointed. There was a tiny ring of color on the cloud, rainbow color. In its center swam the tiny, feeble shadow of an airplane.

Joan Hall tried to smile appreciation, but the pilot had turned away. She thought he tried to hide some apprehension.

Yes! The engine roar was breaking, changing. The plane was sinking in the cloud. The glare was smothered, and dull wisps of fog whipped by. The radio operator worked his key with frantic fingers, scribbled swiftly, showed what he had written; and the pilot glanced at J. G. Hall with somber eyes. The operator passed the slip of paper back; her father read it, nodded—with sick resignation, the girl knew.

She screamed, "What is it?" and her voice was faint and cracked inside her head. She clutched his arm and snatched the slip of paper.

STOCK MARKET OPENS STRONG

But for the moment it meant nothing. She could see the ocean just ahead, lead-colored, tilted, rushing up. The engine thundered just in time; the ocean leveled and swam under. Something touched her hand, cramped on the chair arm, and she turned and almost touched McDougal's face.

He said against her plugged and deafened ear, "Just coming down to gauge the wind," and pointed down at the dull, slow ripples, grinned and settled back into his seat.

Fury swept over her. He thought she was afraid! She glared at him, but he had closed his eyes again.

Monotony. Illimitable sea and fog. There was no land. There were no ships. They should be flying down the coast, not out in the Pacific—hours and hours already. . . . Land! But the plane flew past it, into emptiness again. It was just an island. Where was South America? If anything should happen, how could help find them in that waste of sea and fog?

A strip of green came up and stretched away. Jungle! You never realized how far it reached until you saw it from the air. The plane tipped down. Surely he didn't mean to land there! No, it wheeled and lifted and swung back—backward along its course!

It circled and swung back again. Ranging and hunting—what? Tilting and diving at a strip of water—and there wasn't anything but jungle! Water flew and covered all the windows, blinding the pilot, rushing at terrific speed. What if the plane struck something? But it slowed and settled, and the windows cleared. She saw a sliding, rocking forest, sinister with shadows and black mud.

McDougal's voice said faintly in her ear, "Want to get up and stretch?"

He slid the hatch back and stood up. She tried to stand, but her strained muscles failed her. He reached in and hauled her up and held her—grinning! He plucked the cotton from her ears and said, "Relax. Smoke if you want to, Tom says. Ease your nerves."

Her voice was loud and toneless in her head, saying with fury, "Thank you, my nerves are quite all right." He grinned and touched her cramped and stiffened fingers. Joan Hall snatched her hand away, croaking, "What are we landing here for?"

"Out of gas, I reckon. Missed Buenaventura in the fog."

Lightly he said it, offering a cigarette. She took it without realizing. Lost! She saw the sliding forest, and she knew how far it reached. Then she heard something. Breakers! This strip of water, that had seemed so glassy, was a swirling river, rocking the airplane, spinning it slowly—sucking it out to sea! She saw the breakers, the slow swell of leaden waves against a leaden sky, mounting and mounting and then bursting, grinding down. She heard them. They had seemed merely ripples from the air.

The pilot called from the nose of the drifting plane, "No bottom here. My anchor line won't reach. Heads down!"

III

There was a rising whine from the engines, and hands dragged her down. She struggled to stand up, to see what happened, and a blast of noise burst in her face. Her hat whipped off. Then she was sitting on McDougal's knee, and wind tore at her hair roots, and she screamed at him, "My hat! My hat blew off!"

He grinned and showed it in his hand. He held her down out of the roaring wind stream at the open hatch. The plane was moving toward the shore. She screamed at him, "You said we were out of gas!"

He turned his face to reach her ear, and his lips brushed her cheek. "Tom isn't taking any chances. Not enough to reach the next fuel station."

"What'll we do?"

"Sit here, I reckon, till they send us a plane with gas."

"Do they know where we are?"

McDougal shook his head, and his voice suddenly was loud; the engine roar had stopped. He said, "I doubt if Tom knows where we are, himself. This coast is all like this."

Her father's voice spoke then, and it was queerly querulous, uncertain. J. G. Hall was always definite, assured. He said, "You mean to say they send out men who don't know how to navigate?"

"He had a tail wind, sir. And fog."

"Can't he read instruments?"

"There isn't any instrument to measure ground speed, sir. You have to gauge the wind by trees, or ripples on the water. Easy to misjudge it by a few miles an hour; and in four hours' flying—"

"You seem to know all about it!"

Malcolm McDougal grinned. "Not all. I've flown this coast; I used to have a plane. But I'm the rankest kind of amateur, compared to Tom. He's boss of this division—one of the best in the business."

"Then this isn't serious?"

"Not a bit, sir. We're in touch by radio. May take 'em an hour or so to find us, but we're in plain sight, and safe. The anchor's holding."

"So are you," said J. G. Hall, "I see."

McDougal grinned. Still sitting on the pile of luggage—most of it Joan's—he still held Joan quite comfortably seated in his lap. She got up hastily. The three of them stood up in the little hatchway, filling it; and she was conscious of her father's bony frame by contrast with the easy, hard-knit body of the younger man.

On the shore, in the shadows, a queer house of straw stood up on stilts out of the mud. A man stood in the shadows, staring, no doubt failing to identify this monstrous craft with what he saw twice a week, a buzzing insect in the sky. The pilot shouted, and he vanished. The pilot said, "You try him, Mac. Maybe he doesn't understand Spanish."

"Well, in these countries, yes. Or used to."

"Tell me about him!"

But the plane was ready. It took off again, sure, steady, powerful, flying along a coast no longer strange, no longer frightening. The girl sat easy and relaxed. Sometimes she met McDougal's eyes, blue in his sun-tanned face, easy and self-possessed. This was McDougal's country. The fog was gone. In a clear, hot sunset the amphibian slid down into tumbled water and went wading up on a steep, dirty beach that rimmed the jungle; but the place was picturesque, not desolate. A little settlement was there, and people welcomed this winged token of the outer world. A man sang out, with the glad hospitality of lonely places: "Hi, Mac! Come to the house for dinner. Bring your friends."

There was a gaunt and shabby hostelry with flimsy walls; her father grumbled, but the girl laughed, "What did you expect? This is the tropics!"

Night came sudden and tremendous on the heels of sundown; isolation shut away the sense of strangeness, drawing people close. Her father went to bed, but Joan walked with McDougal on the beach, in the hot, purple darkness; and the long, slow mutter of the surf covered their voices. Joan looked up at the red stars and breathed, "I love this!"

"Do you?" breathed McDougal.

"What do you think?" said the girl, and stood a moment smiling up at him. A sense of warm and vibrant life was all about her, flowing, beating with a strong and reckless beat. He kissed her, a little roughly. He knew how. She tore herself away and laughed, a little breathless, "We'll be late for dinner!"

port. She turned and caught McDougal's eye—he sat far back now—shaping a question with her lips: "Lima?" He merely nodded. This was no foreign and exciting land to him.

Well, let him be that way! She wouldn't even bother to say good-by. The airplane slid to a ponderous and perfect landing, and reporters crowded up to interview her father, and she posed with him for pictures. Men were there to welcome J. G. Hall, respectful men who did his business but had never seen him. They made much of her. McDougal didn't seem to notice.

Only one man was there to welcome him. That was a huge and awkward man, bearded and faded to a grizzled roan, shrunken and somehow lost inside his clothes. His collar was too big for him. He shook hands awkwardly and rumbled, "Hi, kid! How's it go?"

"Okay, Red," said the younger man. "You're lookin' fit."

The big man wasn't. But his eyes turned idly on the stir of J. G. Hall's reception, and the girl was startled. She had never seen such instant and electric eyes, so clear, direct and blue—unconsciously direct, absorbing what they looked at.

Only a moment; they had turned away. Graciously, though, the girl moved through the hubbub, offered her hand, said smiling, "Good-by, Mac. I've enjoyed the trip. Won't you present me to your father?"

Malcolm McDougal said the words. The big man

grinned and rumbled, "Now I know why he's so absent-minded! I don't blame him. How'd you know I was his dad?"

"Oh, I know all about you," laughed the girl. "They call you Red, and you're the man that opened the Marañon, and you believe you've got a clue to the *peje grande*."

Up to the last two words, the big man's eyes were happy, clear, beaming with humor; but a shocking change came in them. They almost glazed. They shifted wildly, desperately, fixing on one man and another, searching to see if any ear had heard. Suddenly, with a thrill, the girl believed—saw the reality of what had been strange and idle talk, talk to fill up an evening in a lonely house between the jungle and the booming sea.

The big man pleaded, "Kid, did you throw me down?"

Malcolm McDougal met his father's eyes and said, "I told Chuck Searl, Red. I'm a fool. Talking, and didn't stop to think."

"Who else was there?"

"Just Joan." Unconsciously he called her so: "Just Joan." The big man's eyes turned on her, and she felt the massive impact of his personality.

"Did you tell anybody?"

"No," said the girl, and felt a thrill of credit undeserved. It hadn't seemed important.

"Don't," said Red McDougal.

Then, before her eyes, a queer thing happened. Red McDougal wilted. All the force, the massiveness went out of him. He grinned, but it was not the same.

"Don't get me wrong, ma'am. Sorry I was rude. But I— Nobody's business. You see that, don't you?"

"Quite," said Joan Hall.

"No harm done anyway. Nobody would believe it. Many a man has thought he had a hunch, these last four hundred years; I've had a few myself, and nothing ever came of those. Maybe there isn't anything. But there's a chance. I've got to try it. Haven't had much luck, these last few years. I reckon Malcolm told you?"

"Yes," said Malcolm, speaking as to a child. "She knows about your railroad, Red. Come on, let's go."

"All right, all right, kid. . . . Glad to have met you, ma'am. And I don't blame the kid for tellin' all he knows—to you." The old man grinned, hollow, ingratiating. "You won't mention it to anybody?"

"No," said the girl. "Good-by."

Six feet away, a man stood motionless. He hadn't looked at Red McDougal, but he hadn't moved a muscle for two minutes; and he wasn't listening to J. G. Hall. Somebody offered, "Want to meet him?" and the man started.

"Huh? Meet who? . . . Oh! Sorry. Yes, I'd like to."

Harvey, his name was; but the girl forgot. Nobody said a word about Consolidated Oil. Her father's companies were not concerned with oil. The man was medium in height, in age, in coloring—like anybody; easy to forget.

Lima was just a city. Old, of course—they called it City of the Kings, and showed you Pizarro's bones in the cathedral. But Joan Hall had seen cathedrals, and she didn't care for bones. The taxis zipped like any taxis, and the street cars whined, and radios and phonographs howled all night long with no respect for majesty or age. There was a big hotel with miles of corridors and lofty rooms. There was a country club like any country club, with golf links and a clubhouse more magnificent than most. There was a dance in honor of Joan Hall, but no McDougal was invited. The McDougals were not members of the country club.

A man named Harvey told her that. Maybe the name was Carson or O'Brien; there was nothing to distinguish him from other men she met, mostly Americans and mostly middle-aged.

He said derisively, "Sure, everybody knows old Red. Hasn't he been around to brace your father to invest some money in his railroad—or a dime for a cup of coffee?"

VI

J. G. HALL said mildly, "If it's as bad as that, how can his son go flying around the country? Flying's expensive."

"Oh," said the man derisively, "young Mac was raised to be a sport, before old Red's delusions folded up."

"Delusions?" said the girl.

"A pipe dream. Thought he could build a railroad over the Andes to the navigable waters of the Amazon."

"Impossible?" said J. G. Hall.

"Impractical. Expensive. Useless. There's already one railroad across the Andes—Buenos Aires to Chile—and it's shut down half the year. No business. But he kidded the old Dictator into giving him a concession—for the glory of Peru, you know, and Red McDougal's profit."

"And he failed?"

"Went broke. Completely," said the man, oddly with satisfaction. "When the old Dictator fell, he couldn't kid the new administration."

"Canceled his concession?"

"He's still got it," said the man, oddly with disapproval. "Not that it's any good. Nobody's fool enough to put up millions for a thing like that."

Joan Hall surprised her father then. She said, "Isn't there oil along the Marañon?"

"Hooey!" said Mr. Carson, or O'Brien. "That's another pipe dream. Old McDougal's no geologist; he's just a jackleg engineer."

"What do you know about the Mara—what's its name?" said J. G. Hall.

"Nothing," said Joan. She wasn't interested in oil.

She might as well have stayed at home. Peru? It wasn't even tropical. The hills were bare. The nights were cold, the mornings overcast—something about an ocean current flowing up from the South Pole. They talked about the ancient glories of the Incas, but the Indians on the street talked Spanish, and the shops could gyp you just as smoothly as the shops for tourists anywhere. The men she met—associates of J. G. Hall—talked business when they weren't talking golf.

Was this Peru? She knew it wasn't. Even the men she danced with told her that.

"You mustn't judge Peru by Lima. Make your father take you up into the back country. Cuzco, the Urubamba—"

Not the Marañon. These men had never seen the Marañon. Few of them even knew the places they recommended, though they meant to visit them some day when they could spare the time from golf and business. But the words curled on the tongue. Cuzco, the Urubamba. . . . She had seen the desert roll away and break in rising waves against the sky, seen something rise behind them, blue, fantastic and incredible. Peru! Something was there to fit the magic of the name. Two men were out there somewhere, hunting hidden gold—a lean and weather-beaten youth, a great, fantastic, bearded man.

And then old Red McDougal plodded by under her balcony. She almost laughed aloud, so unadventurous he looked. His pace was heavy, weary, and his collar was too big for him, and funny little half-moon glasses perched on his great nose. He carried papers in his hands—typewritten sheets—and studied them as he plodded, risking collisions.

"Mr. McDougal! Red!"

The man looked up without surprise, shuffled the papers awkwardly, took off his hat and rumbled, "Howdy-do."

"Don't you remember me—Joan Hall?"

"Yes'm," said Red McDougal, and no more than that.

"Come up. I want to talk to you."

Evasive, the man replied, "Got to meet Malcolm."

"Where? Come up and have some tea. We'll telephone him."

"He won't come," said Red McDougal, "I can tell you that."

Joan Hall was not offended. She was curious. Not many men refused an invitation from Joan Hall. She laughed, demanding, "Why? Have I got leprosy or something?"

"No," said the old man calmly, "but your dad's got money. Malcolm made me promise to lay off him."

"Oh," said the girl, "your railroad?"

"Yes'm."

"Well," she laughed, "my dad's not here. And even if he were, what of it? There's no harm in asking."

Red McDougal brightened, hesitated, shook his head. His glasses wabbled, and he took them off. He sighed, "I promised Malcolm."

"And I promised you," said Joan, unscrupulous, "not to say anything about—you know. Do you want me to ask you about it this way—shouting in the street?"

He didn't answer. But his eyes fixed on her, instant, electric, queerly like a physical compulsion; queerly she had to brace herself against them.

"Have you already—got it? Or haven't you gone to hunt it yet?"

He searched her eyes and found them obstinate. He answered calmly, "I'll come up."

She heard his heavy tread along the corridor, so slow, deliberate, that it was like a menace; heard his heavy knuckles on the door, two raps, deliberately spaced. She had to brace herself to call, "Come in." Then she was quite at ease. The closer you got to Red McDougal, the less formidable he was—this huge old man, uncertain, somehow lost inside his clothes. He had been bigger once. His black alpaca coat was threadbare at the seams.

He said, "I'd better telephone to Malcolm."

"Do. Tell him to come on over. Tell him I've ordered tea. Tell him," she said maliciously, "my father'll be here in a minute."

He took up the telephone and spoke in rumbling Spanish. He said, "Malcolm?" and began to utter sounds that were doubly comic in connection with a telephone—grunts, clucks, vowels and consonants not in the alphabet, projected from strange parts of the human palate. He concluded, "Okay, kid," so unexpectedly that Joan Hall laughed aloud.

"What language were you speaking?"

"Keshua. Excuse me, but that feller in the office listens."

"Oh," said the girl, "Quichua?"

"Naw!" said Red McDougal. "That's what the Spaniards call it, just because there ain't any *s-h* sound in Spanish. It ain't *Quichua,* it's *Keshua.* It ain't *pampa* and ain't *bamba,* but the Spaniards couldn't hit between a *b* and a *p*. They write it both ways. In this country, most of the time, they call it bamba—'Urubamba.' "

"Say that again," said Joan.

"Say what?"

Joan Hall, feeling new uses for her tongue, said, "Urubamba. Urubamba," and the big man grinned.

"That's right. Not *b,* not *p*. You could learn Keshua. Plenty of people can't; can't hear the difference. Try *tampu,* house. Not *o,* not *u*."

"Tam-bpou."

"Pretty close. Try 'Tampu Toccu'—House of the Windows. That's where the Inca kings began."

She tried. He grinned, "No, no. The Spaniards write it double *c,* but it ain't *c,* nor *k*. Just squeeze it from your throat. Try *kkenkko,* 'cripple—man who walks crooked.' "

"You," she laughed, "are walking crooked—trying to take my mind off! Tell me about this treasure hunt. Haven't you started yet?"

He seemed surprised. He said, "Why, no. You can't go down the Urubamba in the rainy season."

Joan Hall said, "The—" Instantly she checked herself. This big, simple, old fellow didn't realize that he was telling her. The Urubamba! Instantly she shifted: "—rainy season?"

"Yes'm. It's always dry down here; but that's on the Amazon slope, and when it rains, it rains. There's a railroad down as far as Machu Picchu, but—"

The girl said, "Machu Picchu?" That was a name she'd heard pronounced, but not like that.

"Yes'm. It means 'Old Rubbish Heap.' A peak inside the canyon of the Urubamba."

"Aren't there Inca ruins there?"

"Inca, pre-Inca. That's where the House of Windows is. Lord knows how old. Stone temples on a peak, two thousand feet above the river; white men traveled down that gorge four hundred years before they knew the place was there. These other peaks stand up around it, hide it from everything but the sky."

That was Peru. His blue, electric eyes remembered, and she saw it. And her father came. She cried. "You've got to take me up into the back country!"

J. G. Hall said wearily, "What for?"

"To see it!"

"Cuzco, anyway," said Red McDougal. "There's a railroad, and it's worth the trouble."

"And the canyon of the Urubamba!" said the girl.

"Only a narrow gauge," said Red McDougal, "after Cuzco; but—" He looked at Joan, and looked at J. G. Hall, and said, "We're goin' down that way next week, Malcolm and me. Why don't you come along?"

"We will!" cried Joan.

Her father said, "What for?"

She pleaded, "Tell him!"

"Well," said the big man, hesitating, "if he'll keep it quiet. I—"

"They've got a clue to the lost gold of the Incas!"

"Really?" said J. G. Hall, and smiled; but Red McDougal's bearded face was grave.

"I reckon," he said soberly, "I needn't tell you who I am. I've seen you with Slick Harvey, and I bet he told you plenty."

"Yes," said J. G. Hall, indulgent; but the girl paid no attention to the name. None of the men she'd met seemed very slick to her.

"Did he tell you what I do to pass the time?"

"No."

"Got to do somethin', or go crazy. Slick's just got me sittin' on my heels. Well, this is what I do."

He offered the typewritten sheets. Hall glanced at them and said, "I don't read Spanish."

"Likely you couldn't read this, anyway. It's ancient Spanish. Records of the city council here in Lima, early days. I found the manuscript kickin' around a second-hand bookstore, two-three years ago, and gave it to the library; and they want to print it, but it's hard to read. I'm makin' a clear copy."

"Well?"

"And one day I found this."

The big man fished a leather wallet from his pocket. It was long and new, shaped to contain a brittle sheet of paper with a minimum of folding; and the sheet was old, yellowed, covered with faded script—ornate, with many flourishes, but little care for legibility. Hall, peering at it, couldn't distinguish even the letters of the words.

"What does it say?"

"It says an Indian came before the council. Said he was the grandson of a man condemned by Manco, the last Inca—not the last, of course, but Tupac Amarú never amounted to a—"

There was a knock at the door, and Hall commanded absently, "Come in." Malcolm McDougal entered, stiff, reluctant, disapproving. He bowed formally to Joan, said stiffly, "How do you do, sir?" to her father. Then his eyes turned on old Red McDougal, and the girl saw swift amazement gather on his hard young face, a thundercloud of protest in his hard young eyes, fixed on the paper in his father's hand. He opened his mouth to speak, but Red McDougal grinned and beat him to it—

placidly, in Keshua, drawling even those explosive syllables.

He said, "Show neither anger nor surprise. Brave as the condor, cunning as the puma; and be this the same for you as for myself."

VII

An Inca came before the council," prompted Joan.

"Oh, no. That was a common Keshua, long afterward. The Incas were aristocrats or kings. The last one—"

Malcolm McDougal sat down sullenly. He knew the manuscript from which that paper came. He knew the yarn old Red was telling—how the Inca Manco, brother of murdered Huascar, half-brother of murdered Atahuallpa, had escaped from Cuzco, the sacred city; how the dark clouds of Manco's warriors gathered on the hills, fighting their last under the sinking banners of the Children of the Sun.

"Then Manco knew it was all up. The Spaniards had already looted all the temples they could find, but there were plenty that they never found—until it was too late. The gold was gone. Manco had sent it back to Iscacinga—back to the gods that gave it."

Malcolm McDougal listened sullenly. He knew that paper was authentic, but he had no faith in fortune so tremendous; Malcolm McDougal didn't believe in Santa Claus. He didn't believe there was any such place as Iscacinga, but there was a chance. And here old Red was spilling all he knew—to a pair of tourists, a cold-blooded man of millions and an arrogant, spoiled daughter of the rich.

"This Indian told the council that his father's father —great-grandfather, likely; Indians marry young, but they're not much on keepin' count—was one of the porters Manco sent to Iscacinga with the gold. That was considered quite an honor, so it seems. Nobody was allowed at Iscacinga but the men that worked there, and they had their noses split to show that they were sacred. Gold," said Red McDougal, "wasn't money to the Incas. It was sacred—metal of the sun.

"They had no use for money. Everything belonged to the government. Everybody had to work for the government, like slaves. Even the Inca had to pretend to be a slave. On certain days—you know, just ceremony— he went through the motions with a golden hoe and rake."

"Go on," said J. G. Hall, to whom gold might be sacred, but was money.

"Well, it was quite an honor to be sent to Iscacinga. But a kind of an awkward honor. It was a sacred place, and men that went there had to die a sacred death— outsiders, of course, I mean; the ones that didn't have split noses. This one didn't like the notion, it says here. 'He was afraid, and fled, and lived in shame and fear until he died.' It don't say how he got away," said Red McDougal. "Must have been quite a trick, the care they took with Iscacinga in those days.

"This was his grandson, or his great-grandson. It says, '—in shame and fear. He told his son only when he was dying, and his son told his son's son, who now begs protection of—' a whole long rigamarole, meanin' the king of Spain. The notary just put that in," said Red McDougal. "That poor Indian didn't know that much about the king of Spain, or he'd have had more sense."

"What happened?" said the girl.

"He told 'em how to get to Iscacinga, and that's all," said Red McDougal. "There the subject drops."

"Didn't they get the gold?"

"They tried, I bet. There wasn't any council meetin' for a while, and then a lot of regulars was missin'; and it don't say 'absent' or 'resigned.' It just says, '*falleció*. Died. Died,' after their names."

"The Indians killed them?"

"It don't say. This Indian was a Christian—anyway, he knew what gold was for; but plenty of his buddies still believed in the ancient gods. Still do," said Red McDougal. "I can show you churches right this minute with a pair of Indian idols at the—"

"You believe they didn't get the gold?" said J. G. Hall.

"I know durn well they didn't. That much gold, the whole world would 'a' known about it."

"And they gave it up?"

"They thought it was a wild-goose chase, I reckon. And here's why." A thick forefinger pointed: "It says here, 'From Cuzco, City of the Sun. From the old rubbish heap—' in Spanish. But that Indian wasn't talkin' Spanish. He was talkin' Keshua. It says here who did the interpretin'."

"Rubbish heap?" said Joan with dancing eyes.

"Yes'm. He didn't know it was a name. He wasn't a Cuzco Indian; he was just repeatin' what his father said; and Cuzco was a long way off in those days. It still is," said Red McDougal. "Not as the crow flies, but the way you have to go—Mollendo, Arequipa—"

"Never mind," said J. G. Hall. "We know where Cuzco is."

"You know a lot that those old fellers didn't. You know what a *picchu* is?"

"No," said the man of millions meekly.

"It's a heap of coca leaves. Outside of Cuzco, when an Indian hits the trail, he faces the sacred city, throws his cud of coca on a pile and asks the blessin' of the gods, and takes a fresh chew and goes on. They do it yet," said Red McDougal, "if they think no white man's lookin'. That's a *picchu.*"

"I'm afraid I fail to follow."

"Well, you can imagine how they'd feel if a bunch of white men came there askin' about their sacred *picchus.*"

"Machu Picchu!" cried the girl. "That's where the gold is!"

"No, ma'am. That's just where you start."

Old Red McDougal's son snapped, "Where who starts? Are you crazy, Red?"

The girl cried, "Could we? Could we, Red?"

"It's no trip for a woman," said the big man, hesitating, "and I doubt if Mr. Hall could spare the time. It's quite a ways."

"How far from Cuzco?" said the man of millions. "We could save some time by flying."

"Only to Arequipa."

"There's a landing field at Cuzco."

"But you'd have to charter a plane. No sense to spendin' the money, just to save four days."

"That's quite all right. I'd thought of doing it anyway, to see Cuzco."

"Get this straight," said Red McDougal: "Four days ain't a drop in the bucket. If you're pressed for time—"

"He's not," cried Joan. "The doctor wanted him to stay away six months—away from business. Make him go! He can't talk business on the Urubamba!"

"If I'm not too curious," said J. G. Hall, "would you mind telling me just why you let us in on this?"

The big man answered humbly, "You know how I'm fixed. I know the country, and it's liable to be expensive." Malcolm McDougal stared. His father's eyes flicked toward him, instant, blue, sardonic. "Malcolm had already told your daughter, and I—well, I had to let somebody in."

"That's fair enough. How far down the Urubamba?"

"There's no tellin'. It says here, 'Passing so many streams as one may count on twice two hands.' "

"And that," said Malcolm grimly, "takes you somewhere in Brazil."

"Oh, no. You're countin' rivers on the map. That porter must have counted creeks, gullies, anything that emptied into the Urubamba."

"Yeah, four hundred years ago!"

"You don't seem optimistic," said the host.

"I'm not romantic," said the young man stiffly.

"No?" said Joan, and laughed.

"No," said his father cheerfully. "He don't believe in luck—unless it's bad."

Then tea was brought, and they were silent while the waiter was in the room. Most of these waiters understood some English. Malcolm McDougal set his cup aside untouched. If old Red had his way, they would be drinking tea at J. G. Hall's expense for quite a while. Couldn't Red see that they were patronizing him, seeing his great adventure as a lark? They didn't need the money. He was just a character to them—that huge, uncertain, garrulous old fellow. How could they see him as he used to be—dreamer of mighty dreams, bucking the Andes?

J. G. Hall brought out a map and asked, "How is the place identified?"

"The peak!" said Red McDougal. "Iscacinga! It says here, 'Eastward, against the dawn, the peak stands riven to its base.' That's why they called it Iscacinga. That's why the men that worked there had their noses split—or so the story goes."

Malcolm McDougal murmured, "So the story goes."

The girl said, " 'Eastward, against the dawn'!"

"Yes'm," said Red McDougal. "Must be somethin' in it, too. Malcolm remembers. Once on the Marañon—"

Joan Hall remembered. Hot red stars above a beach

between the jungle and the booming sea. A hard young man who laughed and let her go; who sat there now, impassive, scornful. How would it be to see the dawn come up over the Urubamba with a man like that? She saw the Urubamba on the map. It didn't look like much on paper, there behind the little ink marks of the ranges; but Joan Hall remembered. She had seen what rose beyond the desert, blue, fantastic and incredible.

And J. G. Hall remembered. For a little while, an accident had broken through the dry, exhausting shell of schedules, mathematics and percentage.

There was a nameless river in the jungle, and a queer, unfounded fear of death, and a human being who had never heard of a thriving seaport thirty miles away.

They talked, but did not speak again the name of Harvey. Red McDougal saw to that. For he was growing old, and luck had been long absent from his shoulder. He must try both barrels—shoot this chance with everything he had.

He didn't need the map to see the Urubamba, growing, swelling from a noisy mountain stream, roll northward to the Ucayali, to the Marañon—behind the ranges, in the country of his dream.

VIII

Dusk had already fallen when the two McDougals went in silence down the long corridors, entered an almost modern elevator and went out into the noisy modern streets of the old City of the Kings. Behind them rose the ornate modern front of the hotel, named for the Liberator—Spanish; in the asphalted street the taxis swirled; beyond, in the wide, gardened square, a great bronze horseman—Spanish—galloped against the ancient stars. The lonely Indians in the square spoke Spanish. Inca gold and Inca glory were a dim and far-off legend here.

In silence the two McDougals boarded a clanking interurban and rode out across the ancient plain to an almost modern suburb, but the street down which they walked bore an Inca name. The house they entered was a large house, almost empty now. Its old and valuable Spanish furniture was gone. A few glass-fronted cases stood about the walls, built to hold souvenirs of Red McDougal's years in the back country—lucky finds, relics of Inca glory dead and gone; but Red McDougal had sold everything of value. Red McDougal's luck was gone, a legend too.

They were used to silence—this big, bearded man and his hard, weather-beaten son. The empty centuries, the empty land behind the ranges were too great to fill with idle talk.

Malcolm McDougal threw his hat into a corner and demanded, "Well?"

"Well what?" said his father weakly.

"What's the idea of spillin' all that guff to a pair of tourists?"

"Guff?" said the big man. "Maybe it ain't, kid. Maybe the gold is there. Maybe we'll find it—Iscacinga!"

"Maybe. And split with J. G. Hall?"

"That's fair, if he pays expenses."

"Yeah," said the younger man with irony. "I got that crack about expenses. What expenses? After we hit the Urubamba, you and I can travel with a knapsack and a pair of blankets!"

"But a woman can't, nor a tenderfoot like Hall."

"That's what I'm drivin' at. They think it's just a lark—and you let 'em think so."

"Made 'em think so," said the big man calmly. "Tried to, anyway. You think they'd go if they had any notion?"

"Well?"

"I kind of hate to tell you, kid. I thought you'd guess it. You may think it's a dirty trick. You notice I admitted I didn't know how far we'd have to go down the Urubamba?"

"Yeah."

"Well, you know where the Urubamba goes."

"Into the Ucayali."

"Yeah. And the Ucayali?"

"Into the Marañon. Good Lord!" said Malcolm. "Do you mean—"

"That's just exactly what I mean," said Red McDougal. "If we find the gold, all right. If not—why, we'll just keep on goin'. I once get that feller out into the back country—"

"That's a long way round to—"

"Well, do you think he'd go there if I asked him, just to see a flock of land? You know he wouldn't."

"No," said Malcolm.

"It won't kill 'em. Won't be any lark, but they can stand it, with a proper outfit; and he'll pay for that."

"I see," said Malcolm.

"No, you don't," said Red McDougal, and his sun-bleached eyes began to burn in his grizzled face. "You can't remember when I started workin' on this thing. When you were knee-high to a duck. Before your mamma died; and after that I just let go of everything. I knew it could be done. I slaved and starved and sweated—starved you, too, kid, sometimes, but you don't remember—and I proved it could be done. I found the pass. I ran the first preliminaries, had it all on paper when I went to the Old Man—before Slick Harvey and the politicians ever heard of the Marañon."

"I know," said Malcolm.

"And I made the Old Man see it—what a railroad there would mean. I wasn't after money. No, nor oil. If I'd wanted money, I could have grafted plenty. I had luck in those days—everybody for me, and the Old Man backin' me."

"I know, Red."

"All I wanted was to build that railroad. Maybe I can't tell you why. When I first saw that country, all that land just waitin' to be opened up, I—well, I knew there had to be a way to reach it. If the Old Man had held on—I can't play politics. I don't know how. I don't know how to honey up to money, either, like Slick Harvey does. My only chance is to get a man with money out there, let him see with his own eyes. I'm gettin' old. I've lost my nerve. This is my chance, kid—maybe my last one. Hall's got money. He's not interested in oil, nor land, but he's sure interested in gold. The whole world is, especially just now."

"I see," said Malcolm, and his tone was different—remorseful. "I'm afraid that I didn't help much, Red."

"Oh, yes, you did," said Red McDougal, and relaxed and grinned. "Long as you didn't make him mad, the way you acted was just right. Doubtful. Showed him that we were honest, not just puttin' up a job."

Joan Hall that night was a guest at dinner in another suburb, but her father was not present. It was a fashionable dinner; it began at nine, an hour usual in Lima, but not suited to a man whose doctor ordered rest. In the hotel, in the middle of the city, J. G. Hall lay stark awake, fighting the nightly howls of radios and phonographs, counting the seconds till another street car shrieked and clanged and clanked under his window. Figures, schedules and percentages went clanking, grinding through his weary brain. Awake, his brain could marshal them, make them march orderly to destinations; but in darkness they broke ranks and swarmed upon him, whirling, grinding, clanking.

J. G. Hall got up and paced the floor. He had to get some rest, had to stop thinking about business. . . . There would be no street cars on the Urubamba.

Joan that night was stimulated, not with alcohol. The dinner was just a dinner. The people were just people, ill-assorted, all in Peru on business; few of them were young. Her partner was a solemn youth in spectacles, a little heavy, something in a bank. He knew her father, and he treated her with great respect.

He said, "What do you think of Peru, Miss Hall?"

Joan laughed and answered, "I could be arrested if I told you."

Loyal to his bank, the youth explained. "You mustn't judge by first impressions. People expect it to be tropical; it's not. Oh, in the north, of course, and on the Amazon side; but on the coast— It's the Humboldt current. There's a lot of desert, but the land is really quite rich. Long-staple cotton—"

Joan wasn't interested in cotton, but she had some skill in the art of avoiding boredom. Her clear, arrogant young face was turned attentively, her red-brown eyes fixed brightly on him, leaving her free to follow her own thoughts. The Amazon. The Urubamba. What was the word for Split-Nose? "Eastward, against the dawn—" The Andes, blue, fantastic and incredible.

Lima was not Peru. Even this stodgy youth admitted that: "Cuzco," he said. "You haven't been there?"

"No," said Joan, adding maliciously, "have you?"

"Well, no. I mean to go, of course, but I haven't found the time. They say it's marvelous. The Inca ruins there—"

"Pre-Inca, aren't they?"

He didn't know. He tried to regain his feeling of authority. He said, "If you go to Cuzco, by all means go down to Machu Picchu." He pronounced it flatly; Joan remembered how old Red McDougal had pronounced it. He said learnedly, "That's north of Cuzco, in the canyon of the Urubamba. Do you know what Urubamba means? It means, 'The Flat Place where Caterpillars Live.' "

"I thought it was a canyon," said the girl.

"It is," said the youth, confused.

"If you know Keshua," said Joan, "what's the word for 'Split-Nose'? I've been trying to remember."

But of course he didn't know. It was a man three places down the table who replied, smiling, "The word is Iscacinga. So you've heard the legend?"

"Yes."

"You must have heard it from some old-timer. I notice you call the language Keshua, not Quichua. That's very technical."

"I did," laughed Joan. "A very picturesque old-timer—Red McDougal. Know him?"

"Sure," said the man, indulgent. "Everybody knows old Red. He used to be quite a fellow, but he's down and out. How did you happen to meet him?"

The girl said lightly, "He's going to guide us on a trip into the back country. A good guide, isn't he?"

"Guide?" said the man. But smoothly, instantly, as if it qualified his answer, he inquired, "What part of the back country?"

"The Urubamba," said the girl, and liked the flavor of the name.

That was all right. She didn't say a word about the *peje grande,* the lost gold of the Incas. The man was one who had been properly presented somewhere—Carson, O'Brien, Harvey—one of those ordinary names. Nothing spectacular or sinister about him; he was medium in height, in age, in coloring—just one of those men you met in a company of strangers. Joan was really talking to herself. Her father's money had provided the best tutors for her bridge, her golf, her swimming, but she had no training in the art of keeping the human mouth shut.

IX

NOTHING to hide about a trip to Cuzco, even to Machu Picchu; many a tourist went that far. Not many, though, had such a guide as Red McDougal—that huge, bearded, picturesque old-timer. Joan discovered that it lifted her out of the tourist class.

It came to Red McDougal, and he was disturbed. He said, "I ought to have told you not to say that we'd be travelin' together."

"Why?" said J. G. Hall.

"People are used to seein' me hit out for the back country, but they'll notice if I've got a man like you along."

"Why not?" said the man of millions, used to moving in publicity.

"They know I ain't a guide exactly. If they guess how far we're goin', they'll know somethin's up; and if they guess what we're after—"

"Hell!" said J. G. Hall, fretful with radios and phonographs and street cars. "If I choose to take a trip into the country, it's nobody's business."

Red McDougal dared not answer that in full. He merely said, "No, but I ain't the only man that ever heard of Inca gold. . . . Reckon you didn't mention that, Miss Joan?"

The girl denied it, truthfully. The accusation thrilled her, and the myth took on reality.

"Oh, well," said the big man, "maybe no harm's done. But we better not lay in our outfit here. We'll act like we're just goin' down to Machu Picchu. I'll wire Charley Farr to meet us there with an outfit. Charley's a miner. He's a good prospector, and we ought to have one with us. If we don't find the gold they hid, we may find Iscacinga—where it came from."

Malcolm McDougal asked the girl, "Have you got riding clothes along?"

"Of course," said Joan, who had all kinds of clothes along—of course.

"What kind of boots?"

"Riding, of course."

"No good. They'll rub your heels and tire your ankles when we have to walk; and we're sure to have to, sometimes. Are you game?"

"Of course," said Joan, who had never walked except from choice. The prospect challenged her; she laughed.

"Good gal," said Malcolm. "Get some hiking boots. Not by the dozen, though; don't make a fuss about it. Get me? And be sure they fit."

Surely no tourists ever had such a pair of guides. The big man was respectful, diffident; his son was easy, flippant, sophisticated, treating her as an equal, when he wasn't condescending. That was a challenge too. Joan Hall remembered. She would tame the fellow—out on the Urubamba, in the jungle, under the hot red stars.

They went by airplane to Arequipa. Red McDougal, who had never flown, resisted; but her father flatly refused to waste three days by boat and train to reach a point that could be reached in four and a half hours. Time was the one thing J. G. Hall had never wasted.

Again Joan saw the desert roll away and break in mighty waves against the sky. She saw the snow-capped cone of Misti, mighty outpost of the Andes, looming above a quaint and quiet city. This already was Peru! The air was thin, exhilarating. Quaint and comic beasts of burden plodded through cobbled streets—llamas, with looping necks and silly, scornful faces, like diminutive and humpless camels. There was a quaint and quiet hostelry presided over by an elderly and dictatory woman, an American, who didn't know that J. G. Hall was J. G. Hall. His daughter was amused.

A dusty little train went toiling, toiling up an endless, tilted plain, rocky and dry; the sun was suffocating, the air thin and hard to breathe. Her father's face was red; he lay with eyes closed, panting. Joan cried out in sudden and intolerable anger. "You didn't tell us it would be like this!"

"Hold everything," said Malcolm, soothing. "It's the altitude. Relax."

"Your dad's all right," said Red McDougal. "I been watchin' him. It won't be long; we're goin' down already."

Malcolm, speaking as to a child, said, "Think what a job it was to build this railroad. . . . Look—vicuñas!"

Far and tiny on the plain, three slender animals were fleeing, graceful and fleet as deer, but with queer, limber necks. They faded. Joan said crossly, "Well, so what?"

"Lucky to see 'em. Scarce. Can't be domesticated. They've got wool like silk. The Incas used it—royalty. It was forbidden to the common people."

"Scarce?" snapped Joan. "There's a whole herd of 'em."

"Those are just llamas. Look! There's a vicuña. Watch him go!"

Joan watched. Against her will, watching to see another, she forgot the dust, the heat, the altitude. A passenger across the aisle said, "Look, vicuñas!" and Joan smiled with tolerance. Only a tourist could confuse the wabbly lumbering of llamas with the fleet grace of their wild cousins, free on that mighty plain.

That night she walked with Malcolm in a strange and far-off town. The stars were thin; the air was cold, exhilarating, but he told her to walk slowly. Joan felt a sense of conquest, walking on the roof of a continent. The Indians here wore strange, flat woolen hats, not aping white men. Timidly, the women offered little woolen things for sale. Malcolm McDougal grinned and spoke in guttural and doubled consonants; they grinned and went away. They knew Joan Hall was not a tourist.

Now the course was downward, and the land was green. Down toward the Urubamba, toward the Amazon, the country of explorers! There was a valley tilted in two directions, and Joan saw the very spot where water, oozing in the grass, divided—flowing here to the Pacific, there to the Amazon, to the Atlantic! Joan was queerly talkative. Malcolm McDougal grinned and said, "Relax. We're still pretty high up. You'll get a headache if you talk too much."

She got a headache. Queerly, though, she didn't mind it. Nervous excitement held her up. The hills rose high on either side, green to the very top, with farms that stood incredibly on edge. How did they work them without falling off? She could see tiny laborers, like insects—men, taming the Andes! A headache was a little price to pay for being an explorer.

Then reaction took her. Cuzco! The taxis swarmed. The crowd jostled. The hotel was in the upper story of the railroad station, and the rooms were crude, bare, sanitary. Joan said crossly, "Hasn't got much atmosphere."

"That's one thing to be thankful for," grinned Malcolm. "It's unique in that respect. You'd better drink a lot of water here. It's the last place you'll dare to drink it without boiling."

Joan had never drunk boiled water. It didn't sound like a hardship. She demanded, "Isn't there another hotel?"

"There is," said Malcolm dryly. "It's got atmosphere."

Later she saw it, and she understood. Cuzco was not much frequented by tourists. It was distant, difficult, the way you had to come, though it wasn't far from Lima on the map. Even an airplane couldn't fly straight over. Two tremendous mountain chains already shut away the world.

The girl recovered something of her sense of isolation, of adventure. Time had slowed. There wasn't a train to Machu Picchu till the day after tomorrow. Walking through the town, she saw great walls of stone—pre-Inca, Malcolm told her—built into modern houses of adobe; but the modern walls themselves were old, already aged in centuries, and they were merely patchwork on that beautiful old masonry of mighty stones, aged in millenniums. He took her in a taxi up a steep, breath-taking road, a thousand feet above the town, and showed her a tremendous fortress sprawling on the height, built of still greater stones, fantastic, like the work of giants in a nightmare.

"How did they do it?" cried the girl.

Malcolm said soberly, "God knows."

They sat on the giant walls, watching the green sweep of hill and valley; and a faint, sweet piping reached them, drifting, placeless. Then they saw an Indian trudging up a distant hill, driving his tiny donkeys, piping. The pipes of Pan!

Against the sky he stopped, and Malcolm murmured, "Watch him."

"What's he doing?"

"Throwing his cud of coca on the *picchu.* Asking the blessing of the gods."

The pagan piping faded in the silence of old centuries. Joan Hall had never known what silence was.

They sat there looking down on Cuzco, on the little town that once had been a mighty city, Mecca of an empire. Malcolm pointed out the ruined Temple of the Sun, a Christian monastery now—patchwork, with canvas walls painted in sorry imitation of that marvelous old masonry, beyond the skill of modern workmen to restore. He told her how the Spaniards stripped it of its golden plates, its golden vessels, its great golden symbol of the sun, by way of ransom for the captive Inca—and then killed him; how his brother Manco, last of that strange, gifted line whose far beginnings no man knew, gathered his warriors on these very hills, fought to the last against the white man's steel, the white man's horses and the white man's guns.

This was the City of the Sun. The quilted warriors faded in the dusk; a thousand camp fires lifted from the hills, studding the timeless, purple canopy of night. The taxi bore them down into the modern town—not very modern; but a band was playing in a spacious, gently tilted plaza under the dominating bulk of a cathedral—Christian, built of the stones of heathen temples. People were strolling slowly; everything moved slowly here; Cuzco was on the Amazon slope, but it was still higher than many a mountain peak.

Malcolm paid off the taxi, and they walked. Joan Hall was getting used to the altitude. He complimented her. He said, "You're going to stand the trip all right."

"Do we go any higher?"

"I should say not. Down and down and down. I mean, your glands are working; you adjust yourself."

Joan felt a sense of conquest. She had conquered heights, and she would conquer the jungle too.

They strolled to the music of the band. The plaza was immense; it swallowed strollers. There was a broad, lighted walk at its perimeter, and there were walks almost haphazard through the shrubbery that filled it. Joan insisted on exploring these.

A hasty movement caught her eye. As they turned a corner in the shrubbery, a man got up from an iron bench, and the light caught his face. Only an instant; he was gone. There was no path behind the bench. Three men still sat there, staring at her as she passed. And suddenly she was grateful for the music, for electric light, for Malcolm at her shoulder. An unpleasant feeling lingered in her spine.

They were Americans. No, North Americans—from the United States. Chicago or New York. Joan Hall had seen the type. Their eyes were cold, expressionless, but something in them stripped the clothes from her body, stripped away the comforting restraints that made life human. And the man who dived into the bushes was the man named Carson. Or O'Brien. No, the name was Harvey. She remembered now. Consolidated Oil. Slick Harvey!

X

Malcolm McDougal hadn't seen the man; he had been looking at Joan Hall. He saw the others, though, and grinned. He murmured, "The new leisure class. The underworld on tour."

"Wasn't that Mr. Harvey?"

"Huh?" said Malcolm. "Harvey? Where?"

She told him. He said thoughtfully, "I can't believe that he was with those fellows. Slick's a smooth guy; he's no thug. Maybe he just happened to be sitting there."

"Why did he hide when he saw you coming?"

"Doesn't sound like what he'd do. He'd just sit there and grin. Are you sure it was Harvey?"

But of course she wasn't. She had seen the man only for an instant, recognized him afterward—or rather, afterward, found herself thinking of a man in Lima. Maybe it was the contrast with the others that suggested it. Many a man must look like Mr. Harvey—unremarkable. Joan Hall had nothing but a swift impression, fading as she examined it.

The others were remarkable enough. Malcolm McDougal, who had spent most of his life in the back country, could imagine other reasons than a guilty conscience why such men might slip into the bushes, even in a public plaza. Nothing restrained them but the fear of jail. What were they doing here? Certainly Cuzco had no booty rich enough to tempt them—unless they raided the churches; that was where the gold was. And they couldn't get away with that. They couldn't hide—such foreigners as those.

The railroad station, the hotel that had no atmosphere, lay at the lower edge of town, secluded by a reach of open ground. Only the house of the station master lay beyond it, beyond the tracks. There were no trains. There was no street; there was no traffic. On the concrete platform, roofless, J. G. Hall and Red McDougal sat. Just sat. The sunlight faded from the wide green valley, and the stars came out, and still no word was spoken.

J. G. Hall had never known a man who could sit an hour without speaking, without trying to make him speak. In fifteen years, since he had shown his skill as a doctor of sick businesses, no man came near him without trying to talk business. Even a luncheon invitation meant that some man hoped to get a thousand dollars' worth of information for a dollar and a half. But this big, simple man was deeply quiet. He knew nothing about business; what he knew was this strange, quiet land behind the ranges. The man of millions sat in a strange, restful state of suspended animation; and the sense of strangeness didn't make him lonely. He was not alone.

His daughter and the big man's son arrived in a taxi, on the road that ended at the station. J. G. Hall could hear them talking, but he didn't listen. He was loath to break that sense of starlit peace.

It was Joan who broke it, saying, "Father, are you asleep?"

"No," he admitted.

"Aren't you excited?"

Drowsily he answered, "No."

"What do you make of it?"

"Nothing."

"Do you believe they're following us?"

"Eh?" said the man of millions. "Who?"

"I don't believe you heard a word we said!"

"Thank heaven," he said placidly, and knew how strange it was to feel no need to analyze the situation—whatever it was.

They told him. He said, "Nonsense." Harvey was respectable, responsible, and J. G. Hall knew his superiors. Nothing was said about the Marañon. There was no oil on the Urubamba, and the search for Inca treasure wasn't business. The only thing that linked those strangers with themselves was a chance resemblance to a man who looked like almost anybody.

"Well," said Red McDougal, "I can soon find out."

He clapped his hands for the bartender, who was also assistant station agent and assistant manager of the hotel.

He sent for the station master, who was the manager. He spoke in rumbling Spanish, and the man nodded and went in and cranked the telephone.

The station master had no sympathy with foreigners who didn't stay at his hotel. He came out grinning. He said, "Don Rojillo—Mr. Red, the prefect thanks you. On investigation, it develops that those men have failed to register with the police. He will report further."

Joan demanded, "What does he say?"

"Says the police haven't got any record of 'em."

"What does that mean?"

"Means they're liable to spend a week in jail. In this man's country any traveler that don't register with the police—"

"Did we?" said Joan, alarmed.

"You bet you did. Age, sex, complexion, where you came from, where you're goin'—and what for," said Red McDougal, grinning. "Many a time I've said it was a lot of hooey, but I take it back. It comes in handy now."

"How do they know which men we mean?"

"Well," said the big man, "in the United States, wouldn't they know if you asked about three men fourteen feet high, and colored blue? That's how much chance those fellers have got to keep from bein' noticed."

"Do the police know where we're going?"

"Where we're goin', yes. What for," said Red McDougal, "no. You're tourists. I'm just showin' you around." He added soberly, "It may turn out to be the truth, at that."

The stars wheeled placidly above the valley, and the prefect of police reported. Red McDougal went to the telephone. He heaved a sigh and grinned.

He told them, "Well, those fellers are off our mind, whoever they are. They're crooks, all right, I reckon. They haven't got any passports. Claim they left 'em in

Lima, but they've got Bolivian matches on 'em. They could pay a fine for that, but they'll sure stay in jail till they get their passports, or get deported."

Malcolm asked, "Is Harvey here?"

"Says not. He could be stayin' at a private house, of course. But even Slick can't buy the ambassador, and that's the only feller that can square the passport racket."

J. G. Hall slept soundly. Here, behind the ranges, he no longer felt the swirling drag of events. In the morning, in the early sunlight, a casual little train went sidling up the end of the valley, chuffing ahead, backing, stopping at the ends of switchbacks while the brakeman chatted with the engineer—under the very windows of the rearward car, so steeply did the little track go curling. Topping the hill, it slid away down a long green valley where it had to dispute the right of way with donkeys, goats and trudging Indians; but nobody minded. The trainmen shouted jests. Once, in a tunnel, the train stopped while they got down to throw rocks at a bull who chose that shady spot to sleep. They did it genially, but cautiously. The bull was wild.

The train stopped often, and stopped long; it carried freight; but J. G. Hall had no appointments, and the hills knew neither schedules nor percentages.

Joan Hall felt no impatience. Everything was strange. The villages were funny. Gray and solemn walls rose on the hillsides; Malcolm told her, "Inca ruins." The train turned down a gorge where a swift little river ran. He told her, "The Urubamba!" The gorge curled and deepened. Hills rose higher, steeper on either hand, no longer tamed by farms. The vegetation thickened, but no human hand had planted it. That was the jungle creeping up. Already she was entering the country of explorers.

Down and down and down! The hills rose higher, higher. Would they never stop? You had to crane your neck to see the sky. The gorge was vast, but the sky was narrow.

Machu Picchu! Joan Hall had to laugh. On a narrow shelf between the busy little river and a towering cliff, three or four flimsy, tin-roofed shanties bore that royal name. Malcolm McDougal grinned and said, "All out! This is the end of the railroad. All there is; there isn't any more."

"Where are the ruins?"

"There," said Malcolm, pointing to the sky.

"Let's go!"

"It's quite a climb."

"Who cares?" said Joan, exuberant.

"We won't have time to get there and back, if we're going to start today."

"Who cares?" said Joan. "Who's paying for your time?"

She meant nobody was; but Malcolm stiffened. He said coldly, "Ask your father if he wants to wait."

It angered her that he should be so touchy, spoiling the moment for her—that self-centered, lazy, red-haired youth. He'd seen the ruins; this was nothing new to him.

Her own hair definitely shaded toward mahogany. She flared, "I'm in this party too!"

"Here, here!" said Red McDougal. "What's the fuss?"

"I want to see the ruins, and he says we won't have time."

"Oh, sure," said Red McDougal. "Go ahead. No hurry. Take us quite a while to get organized; we couldn't get far today, anyway. . . . Go ahead, kid. Charley and me can 'tend to everything. . . . Miss Joan, this is Charley Farr. . . . Don't come back here, kid. Come to the hacienda. We'll stay there tonight."

She saw a little, freckled man who wore a huge revolver strapped at his spindling thigh. His age was indeterminate; but he scraped off his black, dilapidated hat, and he was bald. His freckled cheek bulged with tobacco, but he spat expertly, freeing his mouth for speech. He grinned and bowed, scraping a courtly foot.

"I'm pleased to meet you, ma'am. When I was Mac's age, I'd 'a' bust a gut to climb a hill with you."

Joan laughed and said most graciously, "I'm sorry you're not his age. But he's elected this time, even if he does burst a—blood vessel. . . . Come, Mac."

Malcolm McDougal grinned. A swift misgiving smote her, but she lifted her imperious young head and turned away.

Malcolm McDougal murmured in her ear, "Okay, sister."

XI

It was noon. The narrow shelf ran on along the river, carved from that beetling cliff, but the steel ended. Rock hung overhead, tremendous, menacing, but gave no shade. Joan was already sweating. Not perspiring; nothing so polite. Joan Hall began to wonder if she really liked the tropics.

Three or four ragged Indian urchins trotted at their heels. Joan smiled at them and tried her tourist Spanish on them, ignoring Malcolm. But they only stared. They thought she was talking English. Malcolm McDougal grinned and spoke in guttural, explosive Keshua, and they responded eagerly, forgetting her. Ignoring her! She'd show him.

There was a bridge of logs across the river. It had no rails, and the swift water made her a little dizzy, but she crossed it. Then a trail led down to the water, ended there. Malcolm McDougal said, "Step in."

Into the river they had crossed. She said, "What for?"

"To wet your boots. They're new, and I'm not going to drag you up and down this hill with blistered feet."

And before she knew it, he had seized her elbow, so that she overbalanced and stepped in. She saw the urchins grinning, and she made no struggle; only stood in the water, in cold fury, devising punishment.

"All right," he said, and tried to help her out; but she shook him off. She'd have no help from him.

She'd show him! The trail was steep, zigzagging up into the bush, but it was plain. She kept ahead. The wetting had increased the comfort of her boots, and it increased her fury.

Malcolm McDougal drawled, "You'd better save your wind. It's a long way up."

She set her teeth and climbed a little faster. This was a lower altitude than Cuzco, a thicker air; she was breathing easily. But it was hot. The bushes were not high enough for shade, but they were thick enough to stifle. She could feel her trim, beautifully tailored riding breeches sticking to her legs.

A long way up? The river was already a long way down. The brow of the hill was only a little way above.

But it receded as she climbed. The hills across the canyon rose and rose. The path grew steeper, and her heart began to pound.

The Indian boys, trotting at ease, slipping through bushes while she struggled on the open trail, grinned with respectful sympathy. She cried, "I wish you'd tell these brats to keep out of my way!"

Malcolm McDougal spoke indulgently behind her, and they vanished. Instantly she wished them back. She was alone, weak, staggering with weariness, before that lean, laconic youth with rawhide legs.

He wasn't even breathing hard. He drawled, "Slack up, gal. Stop and breathe. You'll kill yourself."

Joan Hall tried to climb faster, but she couldn't. She could only struggle on. Her knees were water and her pulse was thunder in her ears. He said more sharply, "Joan! Don't be a fool!" She had him frightened now. She'd show him!

Cruelly, though, he caught her arm and dragged her to a stop. She struggled, gasping. "Keep your hands off me!"

"Well, behave yourself, then. No use breaking your heart wide open, just to spite me."

"None—of your business—if I do!"

"Oh, yes, it is. It's everybody's business to look out for idiots and children."

He was laughing at her—that red-headed, hateful, weather-beaten youth. This climb was easy to his raw-hide legs, his leather lungs; he couldn't understand how bravely she had struggled past endurance. Joan Hall cried, "So I'm an idiot!"

"A child. A spoiled one too. You're used to admiration, and you'd kill yourself to get it."

"You—you—"

"Save your breath. Sit down." He dragged her to a seat on a ledge of stone. He said, "It's better, usually, to rest without sitting down. But you're all in. You've climbed a thousand feet without a stop, and you've still got a thousand feet to go."

He was too strong. She couldn't fight him. She sat helpless, furious, his arm about her shoulders; and her heart stopped galloping, slowed to its normal beat. Her fury faded, and she felt dismay. She said, "We're only half-way up?"

"Yes. Do you want to quit?"

"No!"

"Atta old spirit!" he said warmly. But he spoiled it, adding, "It's an easy climb. Many a fat gal does it."

"Oh!" said Joan. "Just nothing!"

"Well, you've got to use your head. Nobody can come up as fast as you did."

"Nobody," said the girl, "but you!"

"That's different. I've climbed hills all my life."

"You're wonderful. You know it all," said Joan. "You talk about spoiled children, but you lost your temper when I reminded you that you were traveling on my father's money."

"I'm afraid I did. That's why I let you overdo."

The girl flared, "Let me!"

"Yeah." He added dryly, "You can dish it out; I thought I'd see if you could take it."

"Well, I'll show you!"

She sprang up and started at the trail. He drawled, "Just take it easy."

Joan Hall took it easy. She had learned that rage would never conquer a mountain. But she stored the fury in her heart. She'd show him!

Malcolm McDougal strolled indulgently behind her. It was safe; there was no edge, no precipice; if she should stumble, she could only roll into the bushes. It was an easy climb. It took only persistence and endurance, and she had them. She had good condition—for a girl, a tourist. But that crazy dash had sapped her strength. It was a real job for her now. He liked the way she steadied down and plugged. That slender kid! She'd do. She had real stuff under her petted, arrogant exterior. She'd stand the trip into the jungle.

On that narrow trail he had to walk behind her, but he saw her profile at the turns—her clear young face, dogged and pinched with weariness. He mustn't let her quit. It would hurt her pride. He made her stop and rest. She did it standing up, in silence. Then she plodded on.

She saw the ruins, ghostly, gray, high on the vivid sky, and her pace quickened. Malcolm warned her, "Steady! We're not there yet."

Joan steadied without hearing him. Unfairly, cruelly, the trail pitched down, rounded a monstrous crag, shot skyward; and the ruins were far off. She'd never make it. But she had to make it. She had forgotten why.

The earthen trail had turned to stone, a sort of stairway; once it had been a stairway, but the stones were broken, scattered, lost. The steps were steep, inhuman. She was whispering. "Eleven. Twelve." Fighting them, beating them one by one. "Ninety-eight. Ninety-nine." If she stopped now, she'd never make it. "A hundred and sixty-one. A hundred and sixty-two." She didn't know that Malcolm helped her. She forgot to count. The sunlight was a furnace on the stones.

Buildings were all about her, and a breeze was in her

face. Buildings? They had no roofs. Green bushes grew inside. The massive walls were carved and fitted so exactly that they held no mortar—standing forever, one great stone upon another; but they weren't houses. They were dead. Only a gray, rectangular excrescence on a hilltop, in the still sunlight, ringed with higher peaks against the sky.

Malcolm McDougal said, "You made it. You're a game kid, Joan."

The girl said listlessly, "So what?"

He drew her into shadow, to a seat of stone. Even the stone of the hill was carved, shaped with tremendous labor, fitted to those monstrous walls; but nothing lived. So what? You thought you had to live. You thought it was fun to live. You worked like everything to climb a hill, to carve a stone—do something; but the stillness swallowed you. Something was in this place, inhuman, smothering.

The sky was beautiful, but it was blind. The mountains never knew that you had climbed them.

Malcolm said, "Pretty tired, huh, kid?"

Joan said, "Oh, I'm all right."

He tried to interest her. He said, "This was the secret city. You can imagine it was easy to defend."

The girl said listlessly, "I'll try."

"This was the place the royal family hid out in the dark ages, after the old empire died—pre-Inca, running back four thousand to twelve thousand years."

"It hardly seems enough," said Joan.

"Astronomers can figure that this place has been here at least three thousand. See that wall up yonder with the three windows? That's the House of Windows."

"Really!" said Joan.

"That's where the Inca dynasty began. Three brothers. Two of them were killed, the legend says, but the gods guided the third one till his golden staff sank in the ground; and that was Cuzco."

"Really?" said Joan, for Cuzco was alive.

"Manco, his name was—Manco Ccapac, the Splendid. He must have been quite a fellow. The first Inca. Queerly enough, the last one was named Manco too. And when he escaped from the Spaniards, he came here to hide. This must have been the place. The Spaniards thought it was a placed called Valley of the Ghosts. . . . The gold . . . the gold—"

His voice came dimly to the weary girl. She heard him say, "The manuscript . . . the gold . . . the gold. . . . They must have brought it here before they took it back to Iscacinga."

But the dead gray walls were dancing, spinning slowly, and the centuries were bottomless.

"Hey! Stiffen up. Hold everything!"

Joan tried to stiffen up. Dimly she heard him shout. Then, dimly, a man stood there, alive—an Indian, but no Inca, and no ghost. The man was panting, and he had a jug of water in his hand. He wore a uniform—part of a uniform. Joan Hall began to laugh. She cried, "Who's that?"

"Caretaker." Malcolm added, "I suppose they keep him here to see that we don't carry off the stones."

It made her weak to think of it. She laughed and laughed. Malcolm said, "Stop it!" But she couldn't stop. He shook her. He was very strong. She rather liked being shaken; it reminded her that she was not a ghost. It helped her to stop laughing. It made her cry, but she felt better.

Malcolm sponged her face with water, let her drink a little—not as much as she wanted, though. She wondered if it was boiled.

He said, "Poor kid! I didn't realize."

"Neither did I," said Joan.

He held her in his arms and let her rest; the walls steadied, and the valley was just a valley, even if she couldn't see the bottom. It was very peaceful on the hilltop. After a while she stirred and smiled and said, "Okay, Mac. Show me the city."

"At-a-girl!" said Malcolm.

But the gold of kings was gone. The silent walls were over all the hilltop—palaces and temples, military quarters, dwellings of the virgins of the sun—and Malcolm knew that she was tired. He only helped her up stone stairs to the highest point, where she could see them all. He showed her a great stone artifice, the—what was the word?—*intihuatana,* place to tie the sun, and told her how astronomers could measure the dead centuries that men had used it; but Joan Hall was chiefly conscious of his easy strength, alive.

He led her to the edge and showed her a sheer cliff that fell into a tiny river and a microscopic bridge. He told her, "That's the other side of the hill. That's the way Bingham climbed to find this place. It's the shortest way to where we sleep tonight. Would you like to try it?"

"No!" cried Joan, and her head swam and her knees wavered, and she clung to him. He grinned and drew her back.

He held her safe, and he forgot to let her go. He petted her and told her, "You don't have to. We'll go down the way we came." His voice had suddenly gone husky, and she saw his eyes and laughed. This was familiar! It was just a hilltop in a pleasant afternoon. They were alone. Joan Hall looked up at him and laughed.

He crushed her in his arms and kissed her, and she laughed. She'd done it. She had tamed him—this hard, weather-beaten male, master of hill and jungle. She had tamed a mountain. Machu Picchu? Ancient Rubbish Heap! She was alive, a woman, stronger than space and time.

Malcolm McDougal thrust her off and groaned, "We've got to get down from here."

XII

Joan Hall was gay. She taunted him. She said, "Afraid, big boy?"

He stood a moment looking at her, and his blue eyes hardened, asking a question. That barbarian! He wouldn't play the game. He laughed, a short, sharp, savage laugh. She faltered, "Maybe you're right. Maybe we'd better go."

"Okay!" said Malcolm.

And they started down. He helped her on the long, steep, broken stair below the walls; his hand was hard, impersonal. The steps were terrible to weary knees. Her heart had slowed after exhilaration, slowed to a leaden beat. They reached the trail, and she could see the valley, bottomless, blue dusk already filling it. She saw the awful way they had to go. She wailed, "I just can't do it, Mac. I can't!"

"You've got to. Or I've got to carry you."

No tenderness, no pity. Joan Hall flared at him, "Okay, big boy! Go to it!"

Grimly he bent and swung her off her feet and started down. His grip was hard, impersonal, as if she were a sack of meal shaped like a woman. He knew how—one arm about her waist, the other under her knees, not over them. It made her feel like an invalid. A child. He plodded doggedly, in silence, and he didn't seem to feel her weight. She tried to make herself heavy, but she didn't seem to bother him at all, till she discovered that he had to look over her to see the steeply dropping trail. She twisted till she managed to obscure it.

"Stop that!"

Innocent, she said, "Stop what?"

He set her roughly on her feet. Panting, he said, "I'm easy, but I'm not that easy. When you drop, I'll carry you."

"All right," she said, and started bravely down the trail. Her voice was weak, dispirited. That was not pretense; not exactly; that was the way she felt. But she was cheered to find that it put him in the wrong.

Choking with rage and strain—Joan Hall was not a featherweight, for all her slender looks—he said, "I know you're tired. I know you're used to being carried when you're tired. Or even when you're not! But if you're going to make this trip into the jungle, you'll have to learn to walk on your own legs."

"Then I won't make it," said the girl.

Malcolm McDougal trailed in stricken silence. He'd done it now. He'd let his anger, his own personal frustration, ruin old Red's last chance. This lovely, capricious child knew nothing and cared nothing about land, or oil, or railroads, or even gold. To her this trip was just a lark, a challenge, an adventure.

Gold? To her it was just an ornament. Her father's

money bought it when she wanted it. She didn't realize what gold could do.

And she didn't care. Pleading would only make her stubborn; she enjoyed having the upper hand. She had it. If she wouldn't go, her father wouldn't. She could talk him out of it.

Malcolm said slowly, "Now you see why I didn't want you to make this climb. I knew it was too hard for you. I knew you'd get discouraged."

"Is that so!" said Joan, too tired for brilliance.

"Yes. A climb that any tourist makes; but you've been carried all your life. I knew you couldn't stand it."

"Is that so!" said Joan, and rage lifted her heartbeat.

"And you haven't even seen the jungle yet. You never will. You'll go back to New York and say, 'Oh, yes, I almost saw Peru. I saw a big hotel in Lima. And we started on a trip into the jungle, hunting Inca treasure. But I quit. I got discouraged.' "

"Is that so!" said Joan, panting and stumbling.

"And you'll never know what the world is like. You'll stay in cities, in hotels, in level streets, where cops can stop the traffic to let you cross. Where you can hail a taxi when you're tired. You can't stand being tired. You just can't take it."

"Is that so!" said Joan, raging and stumbling. "Stick around, big boy. I'll show you!"

And her numb legs tripped her, and she plunged headlong into the bushes. Malcolm McDougal leaped. He hauled her out, and he stood her on her feet, and he cursed himself. He said, "I don't know what's the matter with me, Joan. I must be tired myself. I'm crazy. Where do I get off, bawling you out?"

He plucked her off her feet and carried her again; and for a while she let him. It was good to rest, to feel his strength. And it was good to know that even he was tired. When he began to pant again, she said, "All right, Mac. Thanks. I can make it now."

Where had her anger gone? In that dim, dazing moment when she knew that she was falling, and before she knew how safely, it had left her. There had been no time for fright; she only knew she needed all her strength for something real. Something you never learned in cities, in hotels. You never knew how much you needed air until it grew too thin. You never knew how small you were until you climbed a hill. You never knew how useless anger was until you tried it on a mountain. Anger was something that just happened in you when you found you couldn't take it.

And she had to take it. Malcolm couldn't carry her forever. He was tired. The trail was narrow, but he walked beside her, helping her. The sun was gone behind the ranges, and the trail was dim, and purple dusk welled up and filled the mighty canyon of the Urubamba. But they reached the bottom, reached the river, crossed the bridge of logs over the swift water; and she wasn't dizzy now. She was too tired. But she was on her feet, still going.

Malcolm helped her. She looked up at those tremendous cliffs and whispered, not to him, "We'll show you!"

And they turned, not toward the hidden, tin-roofed shanties at the railroad's end, but downstream, toward the jungle, toward the Amazon, the country of explorers. Railroads led to cities, to hotels, to boredom. She was numb, but she wasn't bored.

Deeper and deeper swelled the mighty gorge. It curled about the foot of Huayna Picchu, the Young Rubbish Heap, taller and steeper than the Old One. Malcolm pointed up a dim, tremendous cliff against the stars and told her, "Machu Picchu. There's where we looked down."

And the gorge opened, letting out the sky. They climbed a gentle slope and saw a glimmer that was not of stars. Houses, a place to rest in the wilderness! There was a homely smell of horses. Dogs ran out and barked, a homely, human sound. A door flew open, and her father came to meet them. He was anxious, but Joan laughed and told him, "I'm all right. But oh, won't I be sore tomorrow!"

Malcolm told her, "Not tomorrow. It's the second day that really hits you; but if you keep going—"

Red McDougal, huge, fantastic on the lamplight, rumbled, "Did he run you ragged? Malcolm hasn't got a lick of sense. He don't get tired. He don't know what it is."

"I'll bet he does," laughed Joan, "this time. He had to carry me before I got my second wind."

She'd heard of second wind, and now she knew. Something that opened in you and let out the limit of your strength. But Red McDougal only nodded, taking it for granted.

There was a long, low ranch house of adobe, and a long, low-raftered dining room. Their host, a shy, black-bearded countryman, bowed J. G. Hall to the head of the table. And the man of millions would have taken it, but Red McDougal grinned and said, "No, don't sit there. That's his seat. He's just bein' nice."

And her father humbly took a seat below the wizened, freckled Charley Farr. This was all strange to J. G. Hall, as it was to Joan.

The silence here was deeper than it was in Cuzco. You heard every little sound. You felt the mountains standing over you, quiet, immense, not threatening; they didn't know that you were there. They didn't know your father was important. You could take it or you couldn't take it, and they didn't care.

She was too tired to eat, but Malcolm made her drink a steaming cup of chocolate. He said, "Please, Joan. You'll be all in tomorrow if you don't, and it'll be my fault."

She drank it. Queer, how heat and nourishment could hearten you. As if you were an animal. He showed her where she was to sleep, a little, white-washed room whose central feature was a tall mosquito net. Joan Hall had never used a mosquito net. He showed her how. The bed was just a mattress on crossed ropes, but she was grateful.

In the door she smiled at him and lifted on her weary toes, lifted her weary face in gratitude; but Malcolm turned abruptly on his heel and strode away.

XIII

MALCOLM McDOUGAL didn't sleep well. He was tired, he told himself; that gal was not so slender as she looked. He knew. He'd carried her. And she had taken it for granted.

She was used to being carried, one way or another. She was arrogant and spoiled and self-assured—the daughter of a millionaire. But she was lovely. And you couldn't hate her. She was game. She'd been protected all her life, but she was game.

He saw the corners of her mouth, the warm, intoxicating way she smiled. Sophisticated? Well, she worked a system that just laid 'em dead in cities, and she'd try it in the jungle. She was just a kid. A spoiled one, too. But she was lovely.

Malcolm tossed and turned. He saw a hard time coming.

In the morning, in the warm and sultry darkness, it was he who had to wake her. Old Red simply assumed that he, Malcolm, being young, was her natural attendant. Malcolm hammered at her door, not tenderly.

She said in a soft, sleepy voice, "Who is it? What's the matter?"

Malcolm barked, "Time to get up!"

"Oh! Really?"

"Yes! Really!"

"All right." He heard her soft, uncertain movements in the dark. Why hadn't he gone away? The soft voice begged, "Could you light my lamp, Mac? I can't find the matches."

"Oh, all right," he said ungraciously, and tried the door. It wasn't locked. He snarled, "You'd better learn to lock your door—as long as you've got one."

Viciously he struck a match. He saw her through the dim mosquito net, uncovered, rosy, in pajamas. It was hot, and she was used to having servants in her bedroom. Malcolm snarled, "Well, make it snappy!" and stamped out.

She was late to breakfast. She was fresh and crisp. Her eyes had shadows of fatigue, and she moved ruefully, but she was game. She smiled at him. Her riding clothes were beautifully clean and white. She had an enormous amount of baggage. Malcolm, in his worn and faded khaki, snarled at his father, "Are you going to let her take all that?"

"Oh, sure," said Red, indulgent. "She's a tenderfoot. Long as her dad's payin' for it, what do you care how many pack mules we wear out?"

There was a huge supply of provisions. Charley Farr, who could cross the continent with nothing but a skillet and a few spare plugs of tobacco, didn't often get a chance to travel with a millionaire. It was after sun-up when they got away.

Joan Hall thought it was early. Sunlight hadn't reached the valley yet; it only reached across the sky, touching the hilltops, touching the high and tiny walls of Machu Picchu. Queerly, now, the place took on reality—that city in the sky. She could imagine how it used to be, four hundred years ago. The mountains were so quiet, so eternal, that a century seemed little. She could picture the dark people moving there, the dark, fierce warriors and their dark and humble women. Priests and virgins of the sun. Their Incas, that strange, lordly race whose far beginnings no man knew, so far above their humble subjects that they had to mate with their own sisters.

Manco, the last Inca, hiding from the white man's horses and the white man's guns. Trying to save the sacred metal of the sun. Sending the secret order out to strip the temples, bring the gold to Machu Picchu—bring it from a hundred temples, on the shoulders of a thousand men, and send it back to Iscacinga—back to the gods that gave it.

Here, where this cavalcade moved now—six horses and eight pack mules—long ago, before the days of horses, a long line of men must have gone toiling, loaded down with gold. Joan Hall had never known the lack of money, but she felt the magic of it. Gold!

It helped her to forget that she was tired and sore. And the sun warmed her, and the soreness left her. She had not climbed mountains all her life, but she was used to riding. This was no mettled horse, no flat, trim, English saddle, but she rode at ease. Joan Hall was used to being carried.

Malcolm McDougal rode behind her. Grudgingly he

saw how easily she sat, how gracefully she yielded to the movement of the horse. It wasn't she who slowed the pace. But fourteen beasts of burden simply couldn't move as fast as two. Malcolm and Red McDougal could have covered twice the distance in a day. Malcolm had never traveled with a woman—not in the back country. Nor with such a train as this. His anger mounted as the sun swung overhead. The pampered darling! She imagined this was all for her.

They camped—it seemed to him—not far from Machu Picchu. But to Joan the outer world had vanished. There was nothing but the jungle, crowding, growing while you listened; and the mountains, silent in the sudden sunset; and the river, wider, flatter, fed by many streams, rolling with greater stealth into the jungle.

"Passing so many streams as one may count on twice two hands. . . . Eastward, against the dawn—" Surely they'd passed that many streams already. Maybe tomorrow's dawn would show them Iscacinga! Joan would not admit a sense of disappointment. Could it be so soon?

Old Red McDougal shook his head. He sighed, "I never realized how many gullies emptied into the Urubamba. It must mean real rivers. Iscacinga can't be this close, or somebody'd sure 'a' found it before now."

Her father, practical, demanded, "How, then, will you know when to turn east from the Urubamba?"

"By the peak. The split. It says, 'Against the dawn, the peak stands riven to its base.' That means you can see it from the Urubamba. But it must be north of here—a long way north. This country's civilized. It's a long way to where I saw that split-nosed Indian."

Joan was reassured. If this was civilized! A little fire glowed lonely in the jungle, and its red light glinted on their lonely tents, one for the men, a smaller one for her. The lonely river murmured, rolling into the darkness, into mystery. The stars were red. The mountains were invisible, but they were there. "Eastward, against the dawn—" Joan Hall was voluble, excited.

Malcolm McDougal sat in grim, sardonic silence. She imagined she was roughing it—with tents, with brand-new folding cots to keep you off the ground, with canned provisions, even a man to herd that swarm of mules and saddle your horses for you. And brand-new mosquito nets. She thought mosquito nets were an adventure. Wait till they started tearing!

But tonight a breeze came off the river, swept the mosquitos back into the jungle. Firelight glinted on her face, rosy, excited, lovely.

Joan Hall said, "Wouldn't it be exciting if those men were really trailing us!"

"Oh, yeah?" said Malcolm, for he knew Slick Harvey.

He was wondering how much this gal had talked about her great adventure. Red was worried, Malcolm knew. He'd asked Don Cipriano to send word by an Indian runner if a party came too soon behind them, hiring mules. It was too much to ask that Cipriano should refuse to rent the mules. In these days money was important to Cipriano.

It was important to everybody, except men like Hall, who had so much that it was just a game to him. It was no game to Red McDougal. Slick had buffaloed old Red at every turn. He had a way of guessing what old Red was up to. Slick was slick, and old Red wasn't.

Slick was like the stuff he dealt in—oil. He didn't make much noise, but he was hell to get rid of. If he had a notion what old Red was after—gold, money to build his railroad, cinch the Marañon—Slick Harvey would stop at nothing.

If those men were in his pay—those men who had no passports—Slick would ooze them out of jail. He couldn't buy the ambassador, but he could buy the men who held the keys, poor men, to whom gold once had been the metal of the sun.

There was no means of knowing. Morning came, and they rode on into the jungle.

XIV

DOWN and down and down into the jungle. Civilized? Well, not exactly. But to Joan, to J. G. Hall, there was no sense of danger in the widening valley, in the deepening bush. The days grew hotter, but the traveled trail was plain. You met whole families of Indians, not so fully clothed as the Indians of the cold highland, but by no means savage. Nothing furtive, nothing hostile in their broad, flat faces; only curiosity. They stood respectfully aside to let the plodding cavalcade go by. They didn't presume to speak till Red McDougal or his son gave them friendly greeting.

Always the same greeting, Joan observed. A sort of triple greeting: "*Ama* something, *ama* something, *ama* something." And the timid eyes warmed quickly, and the Indians smiled, perceiving that these strange white travelers were human. They replied always with one series of explosive sounds.

Joan asked, "What is it that you say to them? It sounds like swearing, but they seem to like it."

Malcolm grinned and told her, "Oh, it's very moral. We say, 'Be not untruthful, be not a thief, be not idle.' In other words, 'Hello.' "

"And what do they say?"

" '*Ccampas nocca, jinollatac.* The same to you.' "

Old Red McDougal rumbled, "Shows you they used to be civilized. You can't say things like that four thousand years without it meanin' somethin'. Might not be a bad thing if white people said that to each other every day: 'Don't lie, don't steal, don't loaf'!"

But in the burning days, in the spreading bush along the widening river, Joan saw no more walls of majesty, no sign of a golden empire dead and gone. They passed a few small, squalid Indian villages, not timeless—houses of mud and straw, not set in streets; and some of them had walls of stone, but the stones were merely gathered from the river bed and set in mud under a thatch of straw.

Joan said to Red McDougal, "Civilized?"

The big man answered gravely, "Well, it's been a long time now."

"I don't see any ruins."

"No, not this far down."

"Didn't the Inca empire reach this far?"

"Oh, sure. But the Incas didn't live here. It's too hot for brains. Only the common people, and they didn't build no palaces and temples for the common people. Only the kind of houses you see here. The reason was, nobody owned the land he worked on. He just worked it till they gave him more, or took it away. Nobody cared how soon his house fell down."

J. G. Hall said, "Socialism, eh?"

"Complete," said Malcolm. "Marx was a piker by comparison. Some of these guys that howl about the rights of the common people ought to look into the Inca system—see what happens to the common people when the government takes care of 'em."

"Well," said J. G. Hall, who saw both sides of everything, "at least, nobody starved, I fancy."

"No," said Malcolm. "Do you starve your own horses?"

Joan had little interest in the problems, the machinery of government. The feeling faded—that a line of royal slaves had plodded down this steaming valley, bearing gold. The bush came thicker, more monotonous. More and more seldom did they meet an Indian on the trail. They never overtook one; Joan began to realize that men on foot could move more swiftly than this complex cavalcade. The penalties of being civilized were heavy.

Indians didn't have to drink boiled water. Indians didn't have to sleep under mosquito nets. Their skins were tough, their blood resisted. Generations had bred out their nervous sensibilities. They didn't feel the things you had to grit your teeth and take—the silence and the heat that never let you rest, the mounting strain of slow monotony, the emptiness that sucked away your self-control.

Even at night, when a little fire glowed red on too-familiar faces, you had to keep your mouth shut hard, to keep from crying out, "Oh, this is silly, silly, silly!"

You had to prove that you could take it. Malcolm was sorry for you. He was strong, but you were never quite alone with him. The world had dwindled to six people—

Charley Farr, facetious, cheerful, wizened, all his human feeling sun-dried; Juan, the halfbreed horse wrangler, whose last name you never knew; Malcolm and you, your father and his father. Every one of them knew where you were, what you were doing every minute. Civilized?

Your nerves went raw. Even old Red McDougal showed the strain, took refuge in uncertain, massive silence. Even your father was a stranger. He no longer spoke of business. The familiar weariness had faded from his eyes; they were intent, the eyes of a trailing animal. His thin, hard mouth was set against mere animal fatigue.

In a blazing noon, abruptly, Red McDougal pulled his horse to a stop, flung up an urgent hand, said, "Listen!"

Stupid, the pack mules crowded up until they blocked the trail, and then their stupid hoofs had to be still. You heard it then, a thin, high voice that cried across the sky, drifting down through the sunlight.

Something like "Wee-e-ra-a-a-co-cha-a-a"!

Red McDougal whirled and lifted in his stirrups, staring with sun-bleached eyes over the silent forest at the silent hills behind. His voice rolled out, tremendous:

"*Rimai!* Speak!"

The voice cried thinly, disembodied. It was Malcolm with his younger eyes who caught a tiny silhouette on a distant hilltop. "There, Red! On the outcrop!"

It was not a dying tree trunk on the rock. It moved. It pointed eastward, at right angles to their course. Its voice cried thinly in the silence.

Red McDougal slumped in the saddle, looking at his

son. He looked at Joan, looked at his son and shrugged. His eyes were sick, uncertain.

It was Malcolm then who took command. He filled his lungs and loosed three blasting syllables across the silence; crowded past his father in the trail, spurring ahead, away from the distant figure; and he left the trail and rode in the edge of the river, calling in English and in Spanish, "Follow me. Keep off the dirt!"

Joan, spurring behind him, panted, "What's the matter?"

"Somebody trailing us. Says there's another trail up yonder."

"Why are we riding in the river?"

"Let 'em think we crossed it."

Where a dry and graveled gully ran into the river, Malcolm turned again into the jungle; rode along the graveled gully deep into the jungle. Looking back, he said with satisfaction, "In five minutes, in this sun, they'll never pick up the trail."

The trail of hoofs, wet hoofs, was plain behind them in the gully; but it faded while you looked. The sun would dry it, and the gravel kept no prints—unless some eye were keen enough to catch the scratch of steel on the tumbled stones. Whoever followed them would never know where they had gone.

Deep in the jungle, Malcolm left the gully, spurring up into the crowding vegetation, but his father crowded past him, grunting, "Let me, kid. I'm bigger." And he put his head down, and his big horse plowed into the bushes, breaking the trail a little. Malcolm, behind him, broke it more. Joan followed.

Suddenly her heart had lifted. And the bush was friendly, and the silence too. The bushes clawed, but luckily they had no thorns. Her head was bent so that she smelled her horse's mane, and it was a friendly smell. The horse was strong. His hoofs were dull in the mold of centuries. Whoever followed them would never hear.

Her father spurred behind her, uncomplaining. J. G. Hall was weary, and his aging muscles had no longer the resilience of youth; but years of toil had trained him to meet emergency, to summon all his faculties to meet emergency, the combination of necessity and time. And years of toil had planted one passion in him—not the object, not the end of toil, but the measure of it. Gold!

To him, as to his daughter, the reality had faded in monotony. Now, suddenly, it blazed again. His aging heart beat strongly to the spur of competition. Gold!

The bushes thinned, and Red McDougal climbed the rocky floor of a ravine, up-tilted, open to the sky. And at its top an Indian waited, a brown, stringy-muscled man, his leather cheek bulged on the Indian's cud of coca—that strange vegetable drug that dulled fatigue. He spoke at first in Spanish, but his eyes fixed on old Red McDougal and he shifted into Keshua.

"H'm!" said Malcolm.

"What does he say?" asked Joan.

"It's Slick, all right, I reckon. Says six Englishmen—which means just anybody that talks English. Must have taken him two days to get those fellows out of jail; says they hit out two days behind us. And there must have been two others we didn't see. I reckon Slick means business, or he wouldn't need so many. Good old Cipriano!"

"Who?" said Joan. The name had faded in monotony.

"The owner of the place we stopped the first night out. Where we got these horses. Then they came along, and Cipriano didn't like their looks. Said they were hittin' for a mine back yonder, but they had more guns than any bunch of miners needed. He remembered what Red told him. He's a friend of Red's—and in this country that means friend, not maybe!

"So he sent this fellow out to see if they turned off where they said they would. They didn't. They caught up with us last night, and slowed today to keep behind us. So he cut across the hills to let us know."

The Indian, diagraming with a brown finger, pointed up the hill. The big man spoke persuasively. The Indian shook his head and shrank away.

"Oh, well!" said Red McDougal. "We can find it."

"Huh?" said Malcolm, who had not been listening. "Find what?"

"The trail. Says we can take it, but he won't."

"Why not?" said Malcolm, and his heart-beat lifted.

Red McDougal's deep voice shook a little. He said soberly, "I don't believe he knows. Just scared, that's all. I've got a notion it's the trail to Iscacinga."

XV

EVEN the man of millions noticed how he slurred that last word, mispronounced it, so that the Indian paid no heed, assumed it was a word in English. Juan, the halfbreed wrangler, sat his horse at a respectful distance. Red McDougal called to him, "There is another trail on the other side of the mountain. Do you think we can find it?"

The halfbreed said, "Why not?" and shrugged.

But the Indian stood and watched them ride away, as if they rode into eternity—Joan thought.

There was no trail. The bushes thinned and vanished, and the horses climbed on solid rock. But Red McDougal seemed to know the way. He turned this way and that among the crags; and a pass opened, and the slope was downward, steeply downward into bushes, into the shadows of a bottomless ravine. He said, "This must be it!" and turned in the bushes, riding along the slope.

There was no trail, no sign of travel; only a narrow shelf in the bushes offered foothold to the horses; but the big man plowed ahead. The sun was gone behind the hilltop they had crossed.

The slope was downward. Suddenly, in the shadows, walls of stone stood up above the bushes—human walls, angled against the slope, but built in level courses—built by human hands. And there, beyond them, suddenly, the shelf ended, and a rocky cliff shot skyward, fell a thousand feet into purple shadows; and the bush was purple moss in the deep shadows. On the cliff, twisting and disappearing, was the work of human hands—a stairway cut in the solid rock, climbing and disappearing in the blue.

Old Red McDougal said in a weak, shaking voice, "I got no right to tell you we got to try it. But it's either that or quit. It's a dead cinch they never built those stairs for vegetables or lumber. It's a cinch this house here wasn't no watch tower. It's too low. It was for somethin' they brought down these steps—from Iscacinga! Me, I got to try it. Me, I'd never sleep another wink. . . . You stay here, Hall. . . . And you, Miss Joan. I'll have one shot at it, or bust."

He spurred his horse at the narrow stairway. Malcolm shouted, "Red! Don't be a fool," and launched his own horse into the way and blocked it. Panting, he said, "You can't turn a horse around on that chicken ladder. What if you hit a break? I'll have a look first."

He dismounted and went leaping up the twisting steps, out over empty space. Joan shut her eyes. Where was he? Had he fallen? No, her father and his father made no outcry. Presently he reappeared, far up, not where she looked for him. He disappeared again, still climbing; and the shadows crept.

Then he came into view, descending—trotting! She could hear the jingle of his spurs; his feet came oddly sidewise. He reported cheerfully, "Okay. A horse can make it."

Joan was not a horse. She shut her eyes and clutched the saddle. It pitched sharply upward, and the hoofs were loud, clawing and scrambling. She could feel the drag of empty space, a thousand feet down to that purple moss, trying to suck her off the cliff. The space between her smart belt buckle and her backbone was quite empty.

J. G. Hall said cheerfully behind her, "All right, Joan?"

"Okay," said Joan between shut teeth, her eyes shut.

No use to be afraid. You couldn't quit. You couldn't turn a horse around on empty air. You had to take it.

Red McDougal said somewhere above, "I told you! Look, there's where they dropped rocks on whoever climbed these stairs that hadn't oughta."

Joan Hall didn't look. She clung and took it.

Then the horse walked out on level ground. She looked —too soon; she saw the edge right under her. She jammed the spurs in, wrenched the horse away. Her heart was hammering.

Malcolm said gently, "Good gal." Condescending, pitying, because she was a woman! Joan felt a surge of anger. Everybody else had made it without a quiver. She bent down and patted her horse's neck with a trembling hand, pretending that the stolid beast had suddenly gone spirited and leaped of his own accord.

There was plenty of room on the hilltop. It was wide

and flat, a tableland. The valley of the Urubamba swung far off about it; and the hills that walled the Urubamba were not single, but a sea, a wilderness of hills in which the valley lost itself, groping and looping.

Looking back, you almost thought you saw the peaks of Machu Picchu and its younger, taller twin, only a dozen loops away. This ancient trail must cut off miles at every loop.

But the Indians didn't use it. Why? They didn't know. They had forgotten. But those ghostly walls down there had power still to turn them back.

There was no sign of travel on the mesa. Red McDougal, staring eastward, saw no split-nosed peak—no Iscacinga. Looking back, searching the hill below, he saw nobody following. Slick Harvey—if it was Slick Harvey—must be down there in the valley, riding away along the valley, missing a trail that vanished in the river, in the jungle. Red McDougal spurred away along the eastern edge of the mesa, cutting the loop.

Trotting at first, then galloping. Joan Hall enjoyed the freer pace, the higher air. You couldn't gallop when you had to wait for pack mules; but the big man left them far behind. The sun was dropping. Suddenly it vanished, and the night banged down; but Red McDougal pushed ahead, kept pushing in the starlight.

Then he stopped. His voice was heavy in the starlight, saying, "Anyway, it proves we're on the trail."

The mesa ended, and low, ghostly walls kept watch.

Another stairway dropped into purple darkness, and a platform shelved into the darkness at its head—built to drop rocks, four hundred or four thousand years ago, on anyone who climbed that stair that hadn't oughta.

Men, not horses. Horses might scramble up, but horses were not built to go head down—not in the dark.

"We're stuck, that's all. We got to make dry camp."

Joan Hall had never made dry camp. She told herself she wasn't thirsty, anyway—no thirstier than usual; boiled water left you always thirsty. Tea was better, but she wasn't thirsty. Only restless.

Pacing in the starlight while the men pitched camp, she told herself she didn't feel the silence, didn't miss the liquid sound of a vanished river.

Then she heard water pouring. Charley Farr was making tea as usual. She didn't know her voice was loud, laughing, "I thought there wasn't any water!"

Malcolm said, "There isn't, for the horses. Only the canteens."

That was all right. Horses and mules were tough, like Indians; they had no imagination. Joan said loudly in relief, "Oh, they can stand it."

"Yeah," said Malcolm dryly. "They can."

Malcolm McDougal, too, felt the relief of higher air. But it released a pressure, a control that he had managed in the jungle. Danger was in the jungle. Not from without; not if you had any sense about the jungle. Snakes would get away if you gave them half a chance. Pumas might trail you, just from curiosity, but they were afraid of humans and afraid of fire. There weren't many humans in the jungle.

That was the danger. Living, day after day, shut in with just a few. Getting so used to them that you forgot to be civilized. With just one woman—and that woman beautiful. Joan Hall was sunburned, but her clear skin hadn't blistered, hadn't peeled. The gal could take it. She had been protected all her life, and even hardship was a lark to her.

What did she care about the horses? If they died, her dad would pay. As long as one of them was left, she'd ride it, and the men would walk. Dry camp? She wasn't dirty. It never occurred to her to turn a hand. She sat by the little fire, relaxed and beautiful, and never cared how far the men had ranged on that barren mesa, hunting a few dry sticks to warm her lovely eyes. There was alcohol to cook with, but Joan laughed, "I love a fire!"

Malcolm said dryly, "Did you ever build one?"

"No," laughed Joan. "I must try it sometime."

"Do," said Malcolm shortly.

And her eyes fixed on him, and her laughter faded. Malcolm was grimly silent. That spoiled daughter of a millionaire! She even expected Juan, the horse wrangler, to wash her clothes, and thought she was pretty brave to wear them without ironing. Even on a trip with dudes, you didn't carry ironing boards in the back country.

Malcolm couldn't sleep. Charley was snoring; and the moon popped up, making the men's tent glare. There were no trees, no hills to keep it off the translucent canvas. Malcolm swore. He fumbled for his boots and jerked them on, half lacing them on his pajama legs.

That was another trick about this trip with dudes. You wore pajamas. Malcolm didn't know just why. The gal slept in another tent, of course. Pajamas were all right in towns, but when old Red and he hit out alone, they didn't carry a ton of luggage. They slept in their underclothes.

The fire was dying. When you slept in tents, you didn't need to keep a fire, and you didn't have to put it out on a barren mesa. Nothing to burn. But there was plenty to burn inside you. Malcolm lit a savage cigarette; and the girl heard him and came out to be diverted.

Her soft voice complained, "I can't sleep either."

"That's too bad," snarled Malcolm. "Just too bad!"

He hurled his cigarette into the fire and tramped away. She followed, saying, "Wait. I want to talk to you."

"Oh, yeah?" said Malcolm, tramping.

"Yes. Don't go so fast. The rocks hurt."

"Well, go back to bed!"

She stopped. He had to go back to her. He hated her for that. Her grave, dark eyes were troubled, and her face was lovely in the moonlight, and her slender body faced him in the moonlight. In pajamas. And not even boots. Just slippers. Bedroom slippers, on a hilltop in the jungle! Thought this was a summer resort or something.

Malcolm growled, "Well, what?"

"Nothing," said Joan. Her voice was weak, dispirited.

"You wanted to talk to me."

"I don't see why we're always fighting."

"No," said Malcolm savagely. "You wouldn't know you're beautiful. You wouldn't know I'm human. You keep hanging round and hanging round and giving me a chance to tell you. What the hell do you care if you drive me crazy?"

Strangely enough, the woman didn't seem to resent this brutal talk. She smiled; her mouth was lovely in the moonlight, and she mocked him, "Crazy?"

"Crazy!" said the young man, raging. "You're a damfool kid. You think you're wise—because you've been protected all your life. You can't fool me. I know."

Joan Hall knew, too, and wasn't flattered. Furious, she cried, "You know it all!"

"Okay!" said Malcolm, raging.

And there really wasn't much to say. They stood there in the moonlight, glaring, and the world far off—that arrogant young man, that arrogant young woman. Glaring, he moved closer. Glaring, she would not retreat. He seized her in his arms and kissed her, and she answered, not to be outdone. Joan Hall was not afraid. She knew this man. It wasn't the first time he had kissed her. Anyway, the tents were there, not fifty feet away.

Joan Hall found something lacking. He was strong, but he wasn't humble. Twisting in his arms, she laughed, "You haven't said you love me."

"Do I?"

"Don't you?"

Malcolm answered slowly, "Lord, I hope not."

"Is that so!" said Joan, and twisted free.

He let her go, said grimly, "Use your head. You think this is a lark. How would you like to spend the rest of your life here?"

"What?" said Joan.

"You heard me. This is all I know. Oh, I've been in the States—just long enough to get my engineer's degree. I've met your kind. The daughter of a millionaire! I'm just a novelty to you. But I'm an engineer. Do you know what that means? A hobo. Would you like to live with one? Or do you think I'm going to live on your father's money?"

Raging, the girl said, "What a time to think of money!"

Raging, the boy said, "Did you ever? Did you ever have to? No!"

"Okay," said Joan, "if that's the way you feel!"

"Okay!" said Malcolm. "Go to bed!"

"Okay!" said Joan.

Malcolm McDougal didn't sleep much. In the morning, in the firelight, in the heavy gloom before the sun burst up, he saw her, trim, complacent, beautiful. She didn't need a shave. He turned his back on breakfast, merely because it was away from her. He saw the daily miracle of dawn. He saw the hills turn weary gray, and melt in mocking waves of tender, swiftly fading beauty, lavender and rose and—

Huh?

Malcolm flung up a hand to block away the sun. A little to the left, sharp on the flaming sky, one peak let in a streak of brightness to its very base. Not snow; that was too low for snow. It was not illusion. Mist was rising in the valleys, in the steaming valleys, but the hills turned green, prosaic, and the bright streak did not fade. Malcolm said slowly, "Okay, Red. There's Iscacinga."

Red McDougal straightened. Red McDougal heard a roaring in his ears, a beat of wings. His luck was in again.

XVI

THE difficult, descending stairway didn't drop all the way to the bottom of that deep ravine, but hit a ridge across the head of it; and on the ridge there was a spring, sweet water where the animals could drink. Old Red McDougal didn't like boiled water either. He rode on refreshed. His horse, that was big enough to carry his gaunt weight, was clumsy, but old Red McDougal's hand was deft and sure. His luck was back. It had been famous once—the luck of Red McDougal.

And the trail was plain, disused but solid, cut in the solid wall of the ravine. It was never made for horses, but a horse could pass. It was a little narrow for the mules; you had to watch that they didn't cut the pack ropes, scraping along the cliff. But the mules were nimble. It was safe enough.

One place was dangerous. There was a rising ramp and then a stairway steeper than the others, with its steps more broken.

Red McDougal shouted, "Lead your horses! Malcolm, you help Miss Joan! This is no place to fall!"

It was an excellent place to fall. If you lost your footing, you might hit the ramp, but it wouldn't stop you; and nobody but the condors need have any further interest in you. But nobody fell. He knew nobody would.

His luck was back. They reached the top, and another mesa opened, and the split-nosed peak was plain on the eastern sky.

"That's luck," said the big man soberly. "We never would have seen it from the Urubamba. Never occurred to me that there might be another trail. If Harvey hadn't followed us—"

"You're sure it's Harvey?" said the man of millions.

"Well, it was him your daughter thought she saw. And he's the guy that's watched me and checked up on every move I made, for fear I'd rake up money for my railroad. He's a slick guesser, too."

"What does he care about your railroad?"

"Nothin'. But there's oil on the Marañon, and my concession calls for half the land—if I build the railroad."

"If it's difficult—"

"It ain't! I found a pass at only seven thousand feet."

"It seems to me," said J. G. Hall, "that a truck road ought to handle all the traffic that would ever come across the Andes from the Amazon."

"That's all you know!" said Red McDougal. "Every tourist thinks the Amazon is hell. I've read the books. They talk about canoes and Indians. Hell! An ocean steamer can come right across Brazil. They've done it—warships have. And you ought to see the Marañon. There's room in there for a million people. You can raise anything you want; you can choose your climate, choose your altitude. The valley ain't like this. It's wide. It's wonderful!"

The picture failed; old Red McDougal had no gift for words. The man of millions said indulgently, "A truck road would be cheaper."

"Yeah. But it wouldn't do me any good. I got to build the railroad. That's how the concession reads!"

"The cat leaps out," said J. G. Hall, indulgent.

Red McDougal knew he failed; he knew that he could never talk to money. But he saw the peak, a sign from heaven. As the sun swung up toward noon, the split grew dim; unless you watched it, you would lose it. Red McDougal took its bearing on his pocket compass and proceeded by dead reckoning.

The slope was downward, and the bush came up and hid the peak; but Red McDougal's practiced eye read the topography, knew where to look for passage when the ground broke into ridges and ravines. They came to a sheer-walled canyon where there was no crossing, but he knew which way to ride—the best chance for a crossing.

It was Malcolm, with his younger eyes, who saw those distant, dim abutments on the canyon walls, those twin projections where a crossing once had been. They reached it before sunset, but the bridge was gone. The vegetable ropes had vanished, and the bridge had vanished. This was far outside the land of steel, the centuries of steel. Even the Urubamba was behind them now. All day they had seen no Indians.

Why? Because this was forbidden country.

And the bridge was proof that traffic—important traffic—had once passed this way. Not vegetables or lumber; there was land behind them that could furnish food and lumber for more people than Peru had ever owned. Fast traffic; for the canyon walls were steep, but men could scale them. They climbed down and brought up water for the animals.

Too steep for quadrupeds. The sun blazed up again, and Red McDougal found a crossing and plowed on by compass; and the jungle thickened, and sometimes they had to chop a way on foot. That night they slept in deep, low-swinging forest where they had to chop out room to pitch their tents, unfold their cots and build their lonely fire. That night mosquitoes roared, but they still carried water they could drink unboiled. Strange voices scolded the invaders, monkeys howled, but their mosquito nets were still comparatively whole; and they had seen the highlands waiting beyond the jungle.

Even the man of millions was content, was patient. J. G. Hall had no experience in gauging the watersheds of a strange country, but he had experience in judging men. He followed Red McDougal.

Gold! The scent was strong in all their nostrils now. The very difficulty of the way was proof that something of great worth had been transported here. And what was worth? Even to J. G. Hall, the standards of his life had vanished. Business was far behind. Yet even to this weary man, this aging man, whose body lately had known highlands where the sun was precious and the air was thin, who now knew lowlands where the sun bred life too rich for civilized endurance, there was still one value left. It wasn't money. It was gold, the metal of the sun.

The toil was upward now. And in a blazing dawn, far off, the split-nosed peak rose great against the sky. The valley narrowed, and they had to ride on a narrow shelf against a cliff above a canyon where no water was; but Charley Farr looked down and shouted, "Look! They dug the creek bed out for placers!"

And a near disaster almost stopped them, but it wasn't quite disaster. Charley Farr was looking back, watching the mules, watching the ropes that rubbed against the cliff. A rock fell. Joan Hall didn't see it, didn't hear it; what destroyed her nerves was the loud bang of Charley Farr's revolver. For a moment, queerly, she couldn't breathe. Red McDougal roared in the choking silence, "What is it, Charley?"

Charley pointed. Juan, the halfbreed wrangler, far behind, behind the pack mules, clutched his shoulder. Charley pointed up. His wizened, freckled face was grim.

"I heard somebody. Thought I saw somebody. Somebody dropped that rock!"

But there was only silence and the sun-glare on that timeless cliff. They couldn't scale it. And the trail was silent, and the dust was silent on the rock. How many centuries since men had passed this way?

Should they turn back? They couldn't—couldn't turn their horses on that narrow shelf. And Juan was not much hurt; the rock had only grazed him. They rode on. It might have been an accident. Probably was. They came again to open ground; the valley widened, and they saw no trail, no sign of any human presence.

Only the peak loomed high, majestic, silent in the glow of sunset. That tremendous cleft identified it, linked it with the golden legend of four hundred and four thousand years. But they couldn't reach it; and there was no water in the valley. Water had run there once, had cut this valley, wide and deep and rough—too rough to ride by starlight. Once again they had to make dry camp.

The peak was very near at sunrise; and a spell was on them, riding. The modern world was gone.

The spell of timeless mystery was on Joan Hall. Surely no woman, no white woman, ever had come so far into the past, into forbidden country.

Greater and greater loomed the mutilated bulk of Iscacinga. Scanty brush was on the slope; dwarfed in the scale, they hardly recognized the hut at first—a hut of brushwood, thatched with brushwood, so that it hardly seemed a human dwelling. But a man stood in the door, a human being, dwarfed in the scale of things. A white man, by his dress—white shirt and khaki breeches and laced boots.

Old Red McDougal was dismayed. But he was square—old Red McDougal was. He bellowed ruefully, "Hi, stranger! So you found it first?"

The stranger grinned. His voice was tenor. No, contralto! It was not a man. It was a woman—a white woman!

She said happily, "Are you an archæologist? I'm glad to see you. And— My God, a woman!"

XVII

THEN she said, "Have you got any canned tomatoes? I don't care so much for truffles or caviar, thank you, but I dream of canned tomatoes. With that outfit, I should say, you might have almost anything. But what am I thinking of? Get down, get down! I'm Ellen O'Leary. Do get down. Come in—if you can get in. Did I introduce myself? I'm Ellen O'Leary. I'll scare up a drink —I think I can. I think there's enough. I hope so. No use saving it for snakes. Not now! This calls for celebration."

Charley Farr said warmly, "Bet your socks we've got tomatoes," and went back at once to get some. Charley Farr knew what she meant. Every old-timer knew it. You could stand the heat of deserts and the loneliness of mountains, and the hope of gold could keep you going fifty years, and you could stay alive on almost anything; but you sure dreamed of canned tomatoes if you didn't have them.

Ellen O'Leary talked a blue streak for five minutes and then suddenly fell silent, cautious and constrained. Old Red McDougal knew. That was the way you felt after the shock of suddenly broken loneliness—a little foolish, queerly empty; and you wondered what you had been saying, gabbing away like that.

The hut was a swarm of contradictions. The floor was dirt, but the walls were hung with gorgeous fabrics, richly woven with strange figures—though not strange to Red McDougal. Pumas, condors, feathered serpents, night and day revolving on the three steps of the world. They were royal mummy wrappings.

Ellen O'Leary said, "Don't be afraid. They're duplicates. And they had a lot of sun before I hung 'em."

Joan Hall didn't know why she should be afraid, and Red McDougal didn't tell her.

This was a greenhorn's outfit, yet it had an air of permanence. A bamboo spout brought water from some spring. There was a well-built cooking bank. There was a typewriter on a folding table, and a pile of manuscript. Behind a screen of gorgeous fabric was a shabby cot, well mended, and a man's belongings—worn-out boots, too big for a woman, but not big enough for a big man.

Ellen O'Leary said, "I'm sorry I can't send for Colin. He's up on the job, and we have no servants."

Red McDougal said, "No Indians here?"

"Oh, yes. But we can't make them understand us. They're afraid, apparently. We seldom see them. But they watch us all the time." Ellen O'Leary's face was hard, sunburned and weather-roughened, but her gray eyes suddenly appealed to Red McDougal. "I'm so glad you've come. I—they're quite harmless, I suppose. They haven't interfered with us. But our own men—ran off. They're superstitious. I suppose this is a—"

"Yes'm," said old Red McDougal. "Been here long?"

"Nearly five months. The rains trapped us. And now Colin wants to stay here till the next rains. I suppose we can. But it's pretty horrible to feel them watching every time you step outdoors. Those—they've all got—"

"Split noses?"

"Yes. You've seen them, then?"

"Not here. I saw one once, up on the Marañon. I knew he came from here."

"You—how did you know that?"

"Why, that's what Iscacinga means!"

Ellen O'Leary smiled and said, "Is that the name? I supposed the mountain had one, but never heard it."

"Oh!" said Red McDougal, and exhaled a sigh that almost blew the hut down. "What are you doin' here, then?"

Ellen O'Leary grinned. Her face was thin and hard, but her deep voice was soft, well modulated now, as if she sat in a drawing room instead of a dirt-floored hut; her hand was poised as if it held a cup of tea instead of a tomato can. She said, "My brother's an archæologist. Is that so strange?"

"I mean, how did he get here?"

"Horseback. How does one get anywhere?"

"I mean, if he didn't know what it was?"

"Do you?"

"Where is he? Let me talk to him!"

"He's up on the mountain. Wait," said Ellen O'Leary, "till I finish my tomatoes."

Juan, the halfbreed wrangler, waited for instructions.

Red McDougal told him, "Loosen the cinches, but do not unload. We have not yet decided where to pitch our camp."

Climbing, they saw how Iscacinga had been split by some convulsion of the earth; and water had run through it once, and bridges spanned the split, queerly at differing levels. Men had shaped and set those monstrous slabs of stone. And men had brought them here—how far? The slabs were limestone, but the hill was—

"Oh, my gosh!" said Charley Farr. "My gosh, my gosh!"

The hill was quartz, so deeply flecked with black that J. G. Hall thought it was gray, was granite; and he wondered what those crazy channels meant, dipping and climbing, twisting and disappearing in the rock. But Red McDougal knew—even old Red McDougal, who was not a miner. Gold had been there once, free gold, wire gold, so rich that tools of stone could dig it out, so rich that simple crushing could release it or a simple fire could smelt it free.

The yellow veins were gone from the vast surfaces the eye could reach, and the confronting cliffs were cut in ledges, tunneled and honeycombed; but all the rock was quartz, and nearly all of it was grained with black. It didn't look like gold. But Charley Farr was modern; he knew things the ancients hadn't known. He clutched the rock, caressed it, beat it with wizened, freckled hands and moaned, "My gosh, my gosh, my gosh!"

Ellen O'Leary asked him, "What's the matter?"

"Matter!" howled Charley Farr.

And a voice said above them, "Well, hello!"

A man stood on a ledge, far up; and he spoke in English, but he had no face.

He was all grayish brown. But he did something at his neck, and then his face was white—half white, a mask of grayish brown across his eyes.

"It's ore," howled Charley Farr. "The whole damn hill is ore. It's gold, it's gold!"

"I've wondered if it wasn't," said the man. "Won't you come up?"

And they were grateful for an unexcited voice. A sense of unreality was on them, standing there in the still sunlight, in the riven bowels of the rock, in the dry bed where water had not run for centuries. A hill of gold! Even the man of millions touched the rock, as if his hands might help his brain to grasp it. Ellen O'Leary said unsteadily, "This way."

They followed her like sheep. They climbed a stairway and a ramp along the cliff; and the man came to meet them, saying, "I'm O'Leary. But I see you've met my sister."

And the man was slight, almost emaciated, but his eyes—gray like his sister's, but not hungry like his sister's—had a great and quiet energy. A mask of dusty cloth hung on his chest under that white and startling jaw, and dust was a monotone on all his body, was a mask across his eyes; but the man was happy, you could see. Absorbed.

"Would you like to see what I'm doing?"

In a trance they followed him. No questions, no excitement. Even old Red McDougal, trying to grasp a thing too great for comprehension, was content to follow. There was too much gold, if it was gold; and if it wasn't—

"Ugh!" said Joan, and almost tumbled off the cliff.

There was a wide and lofty portal in the rock, an open chamber. Sunlight filtered past it, queerly misty, so that you didn't see inside at first. What hit you first was not an odor—not exactly—and it wasn't dust exactly, but it clung inside your nostrils, in your throat. Joan Hall began to smell it hours afterward.

"I'm sorry," said O'Leary, "but I thought you knew. I should have warned you."

All about the walls, close-packed, a ghostly congregation sat in attitudes of grisly reverence—their knees drawn up, their fleshless arms about them and their ghastly heads bent down. Not skeletons. More horrible than skeletons. They still had skins, or parts of skins, and some of them had hair. And they all sat in baskets.

For some reason, to Joan Hall, that was the worst—to sit for centuries in baskets.

"Ugh! Is this how archæologists amuse themselves?"

"Eh? Oh," said Colin O'Leary, "I'm afraid we do rob graves sometimes. They buried things. Fabrics and pottery and weapons, and they tell a lot." He lifted a pile of fabric from the rocky floor; and it was thick and soft and intricately woven, but it wasn't silk. "Vicuña," said O'Leary. "Royalty. This fellow was a prince."

"So what?" said Joan, indignant. "Why couldn't you have left him alone?"

Colin O'Leary stared. He said, "This is a coast weave. And look here!" He bent and plucked the toppling head from the mummy whose rich wrappings he had shown. "This is a flattened skull. And the nose isn't split."

"So what?" said Joan, contemptuous.

"Why—why, in this region, none of the skulls are flattened. These are invaders—foreigners!"

"And what are we?"

"Oh, granted. But a long time afterward. Too long to injure anybody."

"Even a dead man's got a right to his own skull!"

"Oh, granted. I've been extremely careful. There's a big job here for an anthropologist. I've kept each skeleton together, catalogued them very carefully."

"And left them in their baskets! That was kind of you."

"The baskets are all alike."

"Not worth collecting!"

Colin O'Leary said, "You miss the point. The baskets were made here. The fabrics weren't, and the skulls are of many types. These fellows came from many regions. Why? And if they were invaders, why were they mummified—buried with honors?"

"I can tell you that," said Red McDougal.

"What?" said Colin O'Leary.

"I believe you got a right to know. You found this place. Your sister says you don't know what it is."

"Afraid I don't. I found it quite by accident."

"Well, this is Iscacinga. Where they got the gold."

"I've wondered if it wasn't," said O'Leary.

"Where they brought the gold," said Red McDougal, "when they stripped the temples. Back to the gods—to save it from the Spaniards."

"What?" said Colin O'Leary faintly. "Where they brought the— Say that again, Mr. McDougal. Please!"

The man was trembling. Red McDougal rumbled, "You're a funny feller. Wasn't a bit excited when we—"

"But if this is where they brought the artifacts— How do you know? How do you know? Speak up, man!"

Red McDougal spoke. Colin O'Leary trembled. Colin O'Leary said in a choking voice, "I never thought of that. I never thought of that. Oh, I'm an ignoramus! But I should have guessed. It may be there!" He pointed a trembling hand at a low black hole in the inner wall of the chamber, broken masonry beside it; and he cried, "Put on your handkerchiefs! Tie them across your mouths. This dust is bad to breathe."

He pulled his own mask up and snatched a piece of wood, a torch, from a small pile of such pieces; and Red McDougal didn't ask him why he didn't have an electric torch. You couldn't buy replacements in the jungle. And the man was careful, prayerful, with his lighter—that small bit of brass and steel and silver. Hills might give you flint, but they would never give you gasoline.

Colin O'Leary led the way into the tunnel; and the roof was low, and the dim torch was muffled in the darkness, in the hanging dust. He hurried on. And then the way was blocked with dim gray cones, the shapes of men who sat in centuries of darkness. Colin O'Leary, bending low, crowded among them, climbed among them; and the dust rose and dimmed the torch and hid the seeking man.

Joan Hall was a little sick, not for the dead men; they were dead too long. This awful thing was not the smell of death. It was the smell of centuries, of timeless dark.

And Charley Farr, inactive, waiting, had no handkerchief. No cry of triumph came. He had to go outside. The sun was sliding slowly in the cleft, sliding from cliffs of golden ore. The rock that he had hunted all his life. A mountain of it! Charley was in a daze. He wanted something in his hand—a pick, a hammer. Then he could be sure. His brain had never met a blinding future, but his hand had swung a hammer, a prospector's pick, for fifty years.

He was half down the cliff before he realized that he could bring a modern torch, electric, instant, to drive back the dark of centuries. The little man began to run. He could be useful, practical—do something!

He retrieved his torch from his own saddlebag, but he still wanted something—something to grip and swing against the thing his mind refused to take. His pick. The pack mules waited at a little distance from the brushwood hut. His pack was on La Negra, a small, skinny, wicked black one. He went toward her, and he hoped she'd try to kick him. That would be familiar.

But La Negra hardly noticed him. Her long black ears were pointed down at Juan, the halfbreed wrangler. Juan lay on his face, but he was not asleep. His face was on a rock. One hand clutched at his neck, and there was a bit of fluff in his stiffened fingers.

XVIII

Red McDougal, who had waited weary years for his luck to turn, could wait no longer. He went plowing after the dim torch, in the choking dust, among those solid, rocking cones. They didn't feel like dead men; they were wrapped too solidly. Buried with honors, after a sacred death.

How many of them? Hundreds, hundreds! On and on the dim torch faded in the floating dust, and Red McDougal plowed, bent double. There was barely room to plant your feet among the cones, and always you stepped over them. How much gold could so many men have carried?

Colin O'Leary said in a choking voice, "Not here."

The tunnel ended. Red McDougal crowded close and took the torch and held his blinded eyes against the rock. But it was only rock. If this had been a drift that followed a vein of freer gold, it had been exhausted. There was only quartz, gray rock that could be worked by modern methods. Gold could be extracted here, millions or billions of it, maybe; but old Red McDougal felt defeat. Colin O'Leary felt defeat. Rock, only rock, where they had seen the metal of the sun!

The voice of Malcolm floated in the dust. Old Red McDougal bellowed, "Yeah?" But the roar was muffled, stifled in the dust, in darkness. They went back. The torch was burning short.

Malcolm said briefly in the dark, "They got him. Juan."

"Who got him?" said old Red McDougal heavily.

"Indians, I reckon," said his son. No use to speak in Keshua, try to conceal it from the women. Charley had blabbed it all.

And so the search for dead men's gold, millions and billions of it, stopped for a man whose life had been worth pennies. Charley Farr, who had brought his tools to test for gold, used them to dig a grave. And Red McDougal, who had never killed a man, stood with a shotgun he had used for years to kill wild animals for food. Old Red McDougal, who had gone for years in safety among Indians, was afraid. The grip of gold was on him, and he had two women in his charge.

Indians were not wild animals. If you remembered that, you could get along. Old Red McDougal was no tenderfoot; he had known danger. More than once, along the lower Marañon, along the Amazon, a bit of fluff had flitted past his face.

But he was not a tenderfoot. He knew just where to look for danger. It was not exaggerated. Indians had to get pretty close to shoot those poisoned darts with any certainty. They had no steel. Their blowguns, made of reed or bamboo, warped. The darts were poisoned thorns or splinters, butted with a bit of fluff—kapok or cotton. They could fly a long way, but with little certainty. The way that thorn was planted in Juan's neck proved that an Indian had come close in the bushes.

And if they came close, you heard them in the bushes, and you spoke. They were surprised to find that you were human. Disconcerted; and that gave you time. And even if you didn't know their dialect, they understood a little, and were curious. And then they called you *Uiracocha*—master, lord.

Old Red McDougal listened. Once or twice he said to Charley Farr, "Wait, Charley. Listen."

Nothing happened. Night banged down on Iscacinga, and the white men—and two women of their breed—gathered in safety in the brushwood hut. They pitched no tents that night. Indians were quiet, could come close in darkness.

But they drew the curtains, curtains of fabric woven centuries ago. There was no glass in the windows, but the modern light gave them a sense of safety.

Ellen O'Leary said in her deep, quiet voice, that was trained in drawing rooms, "Think of having this much light! Thank you for bringing it. If I had anything to read—"

Joan Hall said sharply, "Oh, don't swank!"

"I'm sorry. I'm as nervous as you are. But if they'd wanted to, they could have killed us long ago—Colin and me. I don't know why they haven't."

"Maybe," said Red McDougal, "it's because you're white."

"Oh, yeah?" said Joan. "The conquering race!"

"Not conquering," said Red McDougal heavily. "We double-cross 'em, mostly, while they still think we ain't human. But I never saw an Indian yet you couldn't get along with if you'd treat him right."

"I see," said Joan. "It's Juan's own fault!"

"Be quiet," said her father, trying to control his own tight nerves, to grasp a thing too great for comprehension.

"No," said Red McDougal. "Mine. I ought to have had more sense than to leave him by himself."

They slept that night, or tried to sleep—these seven foreigners, invaders—in a hut that was cramped for two. But they were civilized. They didn't take off their clothes. Their cots filled all the floor. And it was strangeness, quite as much as danger or the crushing thought of gold, that made them wakeful. They were grateful for the sun.

The bush was silent, empty, and the split-nosed peak was great against the sun. Colin O'Leary led the way. He knew the tunnels in the gray-black, golden rock. They tried them all, though Colin said, "There isn't a thing in them. They're just mining tunnels. The only one that was walled up is the one where the mummies are."

It didn't take them long. By ten o'clock these moderns, bearing steel, had traveled all the darkness men had opened through millenniums with tools of stone. Their modern torches flashed on empty rocks. They had forgotten that the rock itself was gold. Their eyes yearned and their fingers itched for beauty, fruit of the toil of generations, the soft, glowing, solid metal of the sun.

They were methodical. By ten o'clock they had explored both faces of that monstrous split, and none of them quite knew that they went faster, faster, panting like dogs on a fading scent. They thought they were still civilized. They saw a reach of water in the further valley, but they weren't thirsty. It was only when they reached the top a second time that they really saw it. Colin O'Leary said dejectedly, "It can't be on the outer faces. Those are dirt, and there's no sign of work."

They stood on the top of Iscacinga, and they faced the sun. The water reached away, not golden. Silver-blue in green, the green of rich, insensate jungle. On that side there were not many hills. The jungle dropped away, descending, dropping to the vast and unknown basin of the Amazon. The water was a lake, slender and long and curving, like a leaping fish. The head was toward you, and an island was an eye. But there was nothing on the island. It was just a rock. Gullies ran down into the water, inlets, forming fins. Even the error of perspective was corrected, and a curving tail was perfect in the distance.

Colin O'Leary said dejectedly, "The lake is artificial. There's a dam down there. Why did they want a lake? There isn't any sign that this was a cultural center. There aren't any temples. Nothing! Indians live down there. I've seen their huts, but not a single ruin of importance."

Red McDougal stared. A dam? An artificial lake?

But it was Malcolm who cried suddenly, "The *peje grande!*"

Big fish. Red McDougal and his son and Charley Farr all cried at once, "Where is this dam?"

"Why, there," said Colin, pointing. "Can't you see it?" Then he comprehended. Colin O'Leary gasped. "I've wondered if they hadn't hidden something there."

"By gum," said Charley Farr, "we'll soon find out!"

But they were civilized. They ran, Colin O'Leary first, and Colin O'Leary was no runner; but nobody knocked him off the cliff. Ellen O'Leary and Joan Hall were left behind, but they were not abandoned. Red McDougal and his son stopped at the bottom, waiting for them. Only the miner and the archæologist went racing after drills, the hammer and dynamite.

Ellen O'Leary led them to the dam. It wasn't much by modern standards. On the eastern side, the split of Iscacinga narrowed and was blocked with earth. Malcolm McDougal turned and galloped down the ancient water bed and howled into the silence of old centuries, "Hey, Charley! Bring a pick! It's dirt!"

Charley already had a pick. Charley had all the tools and all the dynamite the expedition owned. And they attacked the dirt, taking their frantic turns, and found stone under it. No mortar. Only stone, plastered with mud. There had to be dirt behind it. Colin O'Leary gasped, "That's Inca masonry. Late Inca!" But nobody wondered what he meant. Nobody cared. Even the archæologist was not aware that he spoke with reason. If that dam was built at the end of the Inca dynasty—

They toiled like madmen. Charley Farr had brought only a single-jack, a hammer to be swung by one hand while the other held the drill; but they converted it into a double-jack, Malcolm or Red McDougal swinging it while Charley turned the drill. And Charley chose a crevice in the rock, but found more solid rock behind it. Colin O'Leary tried to take a turn, but Charley Farr, sucking a barked knuckle, gasped, "Hey, feller! If you can't hit where you're lookin', let somebody hit that can!"

Charley was civilized. He didn't shoot that educated feller, as he felt like doing. It was noon, and it was past noon, but nobody thought of eating. Animals had to eat; but they were human, civilized. They had imagination. They could vision gold.

It was afternoon when Charley said the hole was deep enough, and sprung it with a tiny charge of dynamite. Joan waited with taut nerves, thinking they stood too close for safety, but there was no noise, no flying rock. Only a tiny "clunk" deep in the earth. Charley went back and stuffed more dynamite into the hole and lighted another fuse. This time he said, "We better git high up, or git behind the hill. The water's comin' through there hell for thunder."

They got high up. They had to see. They waited—endless, that wait seemed.

Then a tongue of flame shot out into the split. Charley had not spared dynamite. One shot or nothing! Then the air split on their ears. A detonation burst the silence of old centuries, went rocking off across the hills, reverberating, fading into fainter and fainter echoes; but nobody thought how far it reached. They watched the water, wondered what that silver surface would unveil.

The water came, not hell for thunder. It piled up at first in the deep split of Iscacinga. Then it poured and filled the split of Iscacinga, rising behind the broken dam, sinking and pouring off into the valley, filling the bed where water had not run for centuries. It simply ran, and nothing seemed to have happened in the lake—that silver reach of blue, of mirrored sky, shaped like a leaping fish.

There was too much water. It flowed off into the long-dry valley, sinking away into the sunset, and its shape had hardly changed. An hour, two hours, three hours. It had a rim of black, and that was the only change that they could see.

Then Colin O'Leary whispered over the sound of it, the changeless rushing of it, "Look."

A point of black was rising in the waters, like a spire drowned in the waters. Taller and taller, slim and gently rounded. But before it showed for what it was, wider shapes of black began to show—thin lines that deepened while they looked, and those were walls. The sun was sinking, but nobody moved. Against the dusk the lines grew deeper, blacker; Iscacinga veiled them from the sun. But they were walls—the bones of temples drowned.

The rounded spire rose over them, presided over their long stillness. Colin O'Leary whispered, "That's a *huaca*—house of the dead. I never saw one so tall."

Colin O'Leary had forgotten now to tremble. Colin O'Leary only watched. The sun was sinking. As the channel narrowed, the black shapes rose in the mirrored, fading blue, faster and faster.

It was just at sunset that disaster came. That black, unmoving spire began to move. It toppled slowly, and then slowly melted in the waters. Only an agitation, a slow, spreading dullness in the mirrored twilight, was a sign of violence. No sound came over the sound of waters; but the spire had melted in the slowly moving waters. Colin O'Leary made a sound of agony, not civilized.

And night banged down, tremendous, cutting off their feeble human sight. Pumas could see in darkness, bats could see in darkness, but their modern torches had to light them down the cliff. They had to find a new path at the bottom. Rushing, sucking waters drowned the ones that Colin O'Leary knew. Joan Hall, stumbling behind Ellen O'Leary, fell in the darkness, felt the insensate grip of gravity, the impact of insensate stones. Nobody heard her fall. The noise of waters drowned her gasp of pain. Her hand was cut, but she was still alive. She struggled up. She trudged, sucking her own blood like an animal.

Like animals, they turned their backs on wonder, toiling to their crowded den. And still no tents were pitched. The night was down; they had to find some shelter.

But old Red McDougal, trudging, bore no torch. He dared not let his human eyes be blinded by electric light. He strained his ears for stealthy movement in the bush; he strained his eyes on every scanty bush that came in range, not of a brute's leap, but of flying bits of fluff—of poisoned thorns.

Joan Hall began to know why men had once worshiped the sun. She knew the highlands where its heat was precious and its light was thin. She knew the lowlands where its heat was unendurable, where it bred life too rich for civilized endurance. Now that mighty eye had looked away and she was blind. Her hand was bleeding, and she stumbled in the dark.

A voice said in the dark, facetious, "Why, hello! Fancy seeing you here."

They stopped, and Joan Hall heard no sound but the rushing waters. Human shapes stood by the brushwood hut. Horses were there, but not below it, where their own string was. These men had come across the ridge from the next valley.

"Thanks for the shot, Red," said the mocking voice. "We might have missed you if we hadn't heard it."

Red McDougal said impassively, "Hello, Slick."

XIX

AND a thing happened in the purple darkness. Iscacinga, looming behind them in the darkness, suddenly was real. Was theirs! The mystery that lay behind it, unknown walls still rising in the sinking lake, a tower that had melted in the slowly moving waters—that was no fevered dream. The queer thing was, they still pretended to be civilized.

Old Red McDougal rumbled, "Hall, I reckon you remember Mr. Harvey?"

"Certainly," said J. G. Hall. "How are you, Harvey?" And he thought he was quite natural about it; thought he had disguised the need to cry, "What are you doing here? How dare you? Trailing us! You think you'll get a cut of what we've found? I'll kill you first!" Aloud he said to Joan, "My dear, do you remember Mr. Harvey?"

Joan said graciously, "Of course. How are you?"

"Oh, I'm well," said Harvey. "This solicitude is touching."

And the triumph in his tone was more offensive than his presence, than the presence of those men behind him in the dark. To Joan, the daughter of a man of millions, insolence was quite as unfamiliar as the thought of danger.

Sucking her bloody hand, she said, "It isn't that we care, you know. It's only that we're civilized."

A voice said in the dark, "Is my face red!"

Her father whispered, "Careful, Joan."

But Joan had never known the need for caution; anger was tonic for bewilderment. She said with irony that matched Slick Harvey's own, "Won't you present your friends? I'm dying to meet them."

Harvey performed the mockery of introductions. One of the men said, "Pleased t'meetcha," and his voice was not the voice of a city man. The others kept a wary and contemptuous silence. They were here for business, not for small talk.

Colin O'Leary said, "If you'll excuse us? We've been on our feet all day."

"I can imagine that," said Harvey, mocking. "See you tomorrow, shall we?"

"I've no doubt," said J. G. Hall, "you will."

That was the hour in which the man of millions and his daughter ceased to be tourists. J. G. Hall had come into this mighty land all unprepared. His companies did business in Peru, but it was minor business, never enough to need his personal attention. He was traveling to rest, under doctor's orders. He had known Peru as a bit of color on the map, a column of small figures in reports. In Lima, in Peru's chief city, he had still been able to maintain that point of view. Respectful men had helped him to maintain it—men who knew him only as a potent name. The force of habit helped him to maintain it; he had spent long hours talking unimportant business, without interest, patronizing.

Now the Andes shut away the world he knew, the telephones and telegraphs and railroads, the extensions of the human mind. The limits of his creature strength shut down on his aging body, measured in inches, not in miles. Even a cry for help would carry not a hundred yards—and find no help.

Yet in his human mind he was not less, but more. His body had achieved the miles, had brought his mind to a blinding vision. Gold! His human courage rallied to the struggle for possession.

In the brushwood hut he said, "What now, Red?"

"I don't know," said Red McDougal heavily. "I wouldn't 'a' put you and your daughter up against a thing like this for a million dollars."

That was the greatest sum old Red McDougal could imagine. J. G. Hall said soberly, "It's not your fault. . . . If Charley's right—if all that hill is ore—this is the greatest find of modern times. Gold doesn't often occur in such tremendous bodies."

Charley Farr said brokenly, "I'll say she don't."

The little man looked sick, his age no longer indeterminate. Charley was nearly seventy, and looked it—that night. On his wizened face the freckles stood in sharp relief. His hairless head was oddly white; Joan oddly noticed that it had no freckles. The sharp line of sunburn ended at his humble eyes. Hats were no mere convention in a land where men had prayed for help and mercy from the sun.

"I'll say she don't," said Charley Farr. "Here I been huntin' gold for fifty years, and I been satisfied with a little vein or two. I don't believe it yet."

"Don't try," said Red McDougal. "Gold won't be much good to us if—"

J. G. Hall said soberly, "You think those fellows—"

"Think!" said Charley Farr. "You ever seen a gold rush?"

Red McDougal said, "They know we're here, and they know what we're after. This ain't on the way to the Marañon. Our one chance is to hope they haven't got a miner with 'em. Maybe they won't know that rock is ore. Long as we haven't found the *peje grande*—"

"But we have," said Colin O'Leary, feverish. "That tower in the lake—there isn't another *huaca* in this region. House of the dead! I don't know much about Peru, but I know Yucatan. The Mayas 'killed' the gold before they threw it in the sacred well—returned it to the gods.

"This was a place of labor. *Huacas* were for burials of dignity. The only mummies I have found were those you saw. Not laborers. They haven't got split noses. Men from the coast—buried with dignity, but not in a *huaca*. Something of greater dignity than men is there. The gold, the metal of the sun!"

Malcolm McDougal said, "I wouldn't talk so loud."

Malcolm was bandaging Joan's hand. It wasn't badly cut, but the disinfecting hurt, he knew. Her eyes were closed, and her small face was white, but she didn't whimper.

Malcolm touched her cheek and said, "Good gal!" when he had finished.

Then he slipped out and listened in the starlight, and he was surprised to hear nobody creeping off in the scanty bush. His eyes got used to the starlight, and he saw nobody. He was not much afraid of open violence. He knew Slick Harvey; Slick was not a man of violence. But if that *huaca* in the lake was what O'Leary thought— Even a man of craft and subtlety might lose his head, go crazy over that much gold.

Malcolm went in, said flippantly, "Nobody there. Slick must have lost his grip or something."

Red McDougal sighed, "Don't get too happy, kid. He knows that we can't get away without him hearin'. You can bet your bottom dollar he won't let us, till he finds out what we know. All he's got to do is watch us in the daytime, and tomorrow's another day."

Ellen O'Leary, cooking supper, laughed and said, "Pinch me, somebody. I'm asleep and dreaming. Nothing ever happens in this place—and now look at the damn thing!"

"Swanking again?" said Joan.

Ellen O'Leary faced about from the cooking bank and said in her deep, quiet voice, that came so oddly from her thin, small body, "Do you mind? I'm getting just a little tired of that."

"And I," said Joan, "am getting just a little tired of being reminded that I'm soft and green. How hard and brave you are. How you can take it."

"Joan!" said J. G. Hall.

Ellen O'Leary said, "That's funny. I was glad to see you—glad to see a woman. I forgot that women got hysterical."

"Who, me?" said Joan.

"Yes, you!" said Ellen.

"Hell!" said Malcolm. "What's it all about?"

"You wouldn't know," said Joan. "You're one of those hardy males, and we're just women, feeble and hysterical."

"Speak for yourself," said Ellen.

"And don't think I can't!" said Joan.

Colin O'Leary pleaded, "Stop it, Nooky."

"Who?" said Joan.

Embarrassed, he explained, "That's what she used to call herself when she was little. Lord knows why. You know how babies get things mixed."

"Oh, quite," said Joan.

"Look here," said Ellen O'Leary. "What's it all about?"

"That's what I want to know!" said Malcolm.

"Never mind," said Ellen. "I can settle this."

"Oh, can you!" said Joan Hall.

The gray-eyed girl stood for a long second staring at the brown-eyed one. Then she said slowly, "No, all I can do is cook your supper. And somebody must."

"Oh, gosh!" said Red McDougal. "What's the matter anyway?"

"Oh, nothing," said Joan sweetly. "Just a bit of female persiflage."

Ellen O'Leary turned her back and went on cooking supper. Red McDougal sighed, "Well, come on, Charley. . . . Come on, kid. We got to pitch the tents."

Colin O'Leary said, "Not in the dark!"

Old Red McDougal grinned unhappily and said, "No Indian's goin' to take a chance with all this fuss."

"I'm sorry," said O'Leary.

"So am I," said J. G. Hall.

"And I," said Ellen. "Look here, Joan—"

"Noble again!" said Joan.

So Red McDougal sighed and rose. And Charley Farr got up, but his knees buckled and he pitched face down on the dirt floor.

Colin O'Leary groaned, "The dust!"

Only his sister knew just what he meant. She knew the little man had gone without a mask into the tunnel where the mummies were. In Arizona, in New Mexico, in Yucatan, Ellen had learned the dangers of old centuries. In Yucatan it was the gas, carbon monoxide. But in Arizona, in Peru, it was the dust that rose and clogged your living membranes, touched your living lungs with fever. Not with germs; not even germs could live forever in sealed chambers. Only the penalty, mechanical, for going back into the unknown dark—for stirring up the dust of eternal stillness.

Charley wouldn't die. Charley was pretty tough, or he'd have crumpled before now. They laid him on a cot, and Ellen went on cooking supper.

Joan refused to eat, said sweetly, "Thanks, but I'm not hungry."

Ellen said brusquely, "Don't be a fool, Miss Hall. You'll be all in if you don't eat."

"And you'll be desolated, Miss O'Leary?"

"Hell!" said Malcolm.

Queer, how a little strain could break the thread of civilized convention. Malcolm ate in savage silence, without appetite. As if it weren't enough that Harvey and his roughnecks waited out there in the dark. Those damn gals!

Ellen O'Leary was more like a man. She got up suddenly, uncomfortably, and went to Joan and touched her frozen cheek and said, "Trouble enough we've got. Make up?"

Unfortunately, however, Ellen O'Leary's hard, small fingers touched the very spot Malcolm had patted—Malcolm McDougal, condescending, masculine. Joan Hall felt very much alone—the only woman in the world, the only person in the world who was afraid.

Unyielding, furious, Joan said, "Of course."

"You'll eat, then?"

"Why?" said Joan. "To please you—Nooky?"

Ellen O'Leary turned her back and walked away. Not far; there wasn't room to walk far in that brushwood hut.

So Red McDougal and his son went out and pitched the tents. With lanterns and with noise. Without much fear.

It wasn't likely that a jungle Indian would come near so many white men. Hardly near enough to launch a poisoned thorn. Old Red McDougal had more fear of poisoned words.

What must the Indians think of this invasion? Colin O'Leary and his sister first, after forbidden centuries. Then four more white men and another woman of the breed. And now Slick Harvey and his gang. . . . The Indians hadn't harmed O'Leary and his sister. But O'Leary's men—what had become of them? Ellen O'Leary said they had run away. Old Red McDougal wondered. Did O'Leary know? Juan, the poor *cholo* wrangler—halfbreed, neither an Indian nor a white man—had received a poisoned thorn.

The moon swam up an hour before dawn, and Red McDougal saw Slick Harvey's camp. The tired old stars went out. The split-nosed peak was huge and real against the sunrise.

XX

PEACEFUL enough, it seemed. The valley gave a glimpse of the quiet forest, veiled with the morning mist; the sunlight touched the seaward hills. The shadow of the peak was opalescent, cool and sweet. Joan Hall came out and stood before her little tent, filling her lungs, unconsciously caressing her bandaged hand. Old Red McDougal was already cooking breakfast; and the smell of smoke was sweet, and the smell of coffee.

Joan said soberly, "Good morning, Red."

"Mornin'," said Red McDougal, and his voice was heavy.

"Oh, cheer up!" said Joan. "We're not dead yet. I'm sorry I made an ass of myself last night."

Old Red McDougal was embarrassed. He said awkwardly, "You got a right to be upset."

"Oh, no, I haven't. I'm just soft and green. But if you'll be patient with me, Red, I'll—try to learn."

The big man stared, said gruffly, "Kid, I'll get you out of this or bust."

"But I don't want to be got out," said Joan. "I think it's thrilling."

Red McDougal looked away, and all he said was "H'mph!"

"Don't you?"

"No," said old Red McDougal, cooking breakfast.

He was elderly, Joan realized; her father, too, was often grumpy before breakfast. Joan was young, and sleep had restored her balance. On the slope, above the brushwood hut, beside the spring where Colin O'Leary and his sister got their water, she could see the camp of Mr. Harvey and his men; but she knew Mr. Harvey. She had dined with him in Lima.

Placid smoke was rising from the brushwood hut. Joan went to the brushwood door and called, "Hello! Somebody up?"

Ellen O'Leary opened the door, said warily, "Good morning. Will you come in?"

"I will," said Joan, "if you'll forgive me."

Ellen O'Leary stared. Her thin, hard face worked queerly, and her voice was husky, saying, "Joan!"

"Ellen," said Joan.

They touched each other—these two lonely women. That was all. For they were civilized, and they were hardly more than strangers. Colin O'Leary said behind his sister, "You are generous, Miss Hall."

"Not I!" said Joan, and laughed.

Colin O'Leary was depressed. He said, "I'd like to offer you some coffee, but—"

"You're out of coffee!" said Joan Hall, and ran. That was a strange sensation—to be running errands. It was strangely satisfying.

She had breakfast in the brushwood hut, and it was

reassuring. Colin O'Leary didn't think there was any danger.

Colin O'Leary said, "I don't see why there should be. If that hill is ore—why, there's enough for all of us. And if that *huaca* in the lake is really the *peje grande*—if that's where they hid the wrought gold—why, it doesn't belong to any of us. I don't know much about Peru, but I'm pretty sure—"

"That's twice you've said that," said Joan Hall. "I thought you archæologists knew everything."

Colin O'Leary smiled, and his gray eyes were restful, civilized. He said, "Oh, hardly. If we did, there'd be no need for archæologists."

"You say you don't know much about Peru, yet here we find you in a place that even Red McDougal didn't know. They say he knows this country better than any man alive."

"Better than I do, surely. I'm not much of an archæologist. Not yet. I've had some years in Arizona and Yucatan, but my achievements have been pretty small. Too small to win much backing. I came here at my own expense. Happened to win a little money in the market, and it gave me a chance to do what I'd always wanted—have a try at things nobody else has noticed much.

"Two years ago an expedition flew over this country, and they photographed some things nobody could explain. Some markings on the mountains. Inaccessible, they said. I guess they are," said Colin O'Leary. "I haven't found them. But—"

He gestured with a quiet hand; the gorgeous, ancient hangings on the brushwood walls let out his quiet vision.

"But," said Joan, "you found the gold!"

"Oh, no. I thought it might be ore, but I didn't know. I thought there might be something in the lake—thought I might break the dam some day, if I could do it single-handed, without dynamite. I didn't have any dynamite. You know, we don't work much with dynamite. Afraid we'll break the things we're looking for."

Joan Hall could imagine that. This gentle, slender man would not work much with dynamite.

The sun swung up, as it had swung a thousand million times on Iscacinga. From the brushwood hut there came a strangely modern sound, prosaic, peaceful—the swift, steady clicking of a typewriter; and Joan Hall was restless, but old Red McDougal was uncertain.

He said heavily, "I don't know what to do. The minute we start movin', they'll be on our heels."

"And if we don't," said J. G. Hall, "they'll start exploring on their own account. I don't see anything to be gained by waiting."

"Neither do I!" said Malcolm, and his blue young eyes were hard, his red hair flaming. "Get your shotgun, Red. Let's go!"

The big man shook his head and sighed, "We got to get along without a fight. One shotgun and one pistol won't be worth a durn if it comes to that. They've all got guns, and I'm afraid they're used to usin' 'em."

Old Red McDougal was afraid. In all his years in the

back country he had never traveled with a woman in his charge, and he had never killed a man. He wasn't afraid of Indians. You could get along with Indians. He had slept in unknown villages where every hut was hung with shrunken human heads, had sat by fires where boneless human heads were turning, shrinking in the smoke; but Indians wouldn't kill a friend just for his head. Even a head like Red McDougal's. Now his flaming beard was grizzled and his hair was gray, but he still wore his head on his own shoulders.

Indians didn't kill for gold, and they had women of their own.

But these were white men, and the pressure of slow, endless time was on them.

J. G. Hall said fretfully, "We can't sit here forever."

"No," said Red McDougal heavily, and rose.

Joan went to the brushwood hut and called, "Come, Ellen, Colin. We're going up to see what's happened in the lake."

The clicking stopped. Ellen O'Leary said, "Thank heaven! Colin was all set to spend the day transcribing notes. The man's not human, Joan."

"Look at my hands," said Colin O'Leary, "if you think so." And Joan saw his hands, and they were trembling; but his eyes were calm. He grinned, "I don't think Ellen has understood a word I've said. My tongue's all twisted."

"So are my fingers," laughed his sister.

They went up, climbing along the rushing stream

where water had not run for centuries; and they were not surprised to see Slick Harvey and his men move after them. Old Red McDougal turned and bellowed, "Hell! Come on, Slick. If you want to snoop, step up and do it like a man!"

Slick Harvey, too, was civilized. He came up grinning, saying, "This is good of you. Lead on, Macduff! Are you going to show us the *peje grande?*"

Red McDougal answered stolidly, "I hope not. We can show you a lot of mummies, though, if that'll do you."

"Thanks, but I've seen mummies."

"Well, that's all we've got."

Colin O'Leary took the hint. He led the way into the split of Iscacinga, crossing the newly rushing water on a limestone slab; and even J. G. Hall could see that Harvey didn't know the difference. He didn't know the rock of the hill was ore. And Charley Farr, still sick and weak, his gaze bent grimly down, was able to refrain from looking at the rock, caressing it—the rock that marked the mighty end of a long seeking.

Only when they reached the open chamber where the stripped mummies sat, and Harvey's men pressed forward, could the little man yield to his sick longing. Charley Farr hung back, pressing his fevered forehead to the rock.

Slick Harvey, staring at the open tunnel, said, "What's in there?"

"Mummies," said Red McDougal.

"Nothing else?"

"Not that I know of," said the big man stolidly.

"You wouldn't fool me, would you?" said Slick Harvey, grinning. . . . "George, you run and bring a couple of electric torches. We'll just have a look."

"You better not," said Red McDougal. "We went in there, but we couldn't stay there long. The dust makes you kind of sick."

"Oh, yeah?" said Harvey.

"Yes," said Colin O'Leary. "You must wear a—"

Malcolm McDougal's hand closed painfully on Colin O'Leary's arm. Malcolm McDougal's voice was loud, anxious and unconvincing, saying, "Take our word for it! Nothing in there but mummies!"

"Yeah?" said Harvey. . . . "Bring a lantern too, George. That'll warn us if there's gas."

"There isn't any gas," said Colin O'Leary, "but—"

"You wouldn't lie to us?" said Harvey, grinning. . . . "Hustle, George. And don't forget the lantern."

Colin O'Leary looked unhappily at Red McDougal and his son. The big man's face was stolid and resigned, the young man's hard, defiant. Harvey saw them all, and knew O'Leary was a timid man. Slick Harvey was complacent.

Colin O'Leary kept his mouth shut. If the fellow knew so much, he ought to know monoxide wouldn't stay in a level tunnel; it was heavier than air. If he thought dust was nothing, let him learn.

The man named George was the only one of Harvey's men who had the look of an old-timer in the hills—a narrow-faced, impassive, rawhide sort of man, undoubtedly the one who did the work around the camps. The others seemed to look with condescension on the hills. They ogled the women and made humorous remarks. Malcolm McDougal had begun to bristle when Slick Harvey said, "Forget it, boys. Business before pleasure."

Harvey led the way into the tunnel, bearing the lantern that should warn him of dead gases, but the city men hung back a little. They were hard in their own environment, but wary of unknown darkness, the wild darkness of a mountain, the grim darkness of old centuries.

The voices of Slick Harvey and the man named George, muffled by dust and darkness, came with rising curiosity, without alarm. The men went in.

Then Red McDougal said, "This is our chance."

They hurried along the ledge. They saw the water pouring through the broken dam, and even they could hardly tell that it was newly broken; and the lake was gone. Only a rim of sunken water grass and reeds outlined the shape of a leaping fish. Inside it, red-black mud lay flat along a wide, flat stream.

But water still surrounded the unknown walls, the heap of stones that marked the fallen tower. Red McDougal sighed, "We got to bust the dam a little lower."

Colin O'Leary stiffened suddenly. He wasn't looking at the drowned walls, the fallen stones of the drowned tower. Habit had drawn his glance to a certain spot, far off. Dwarfed in the distance, at the edge of the jungle where the edge of the lake had been, two upright stones supported a flat crosspiece; and between them, in the hot sunlight, in the stillness of old centuries, a pair of thin, brown human legs kicked feebly.

Colin O'Leary said in a strangled voice, "Another one!"

"Another what?" said J. G. Hall.

"Torture," said Malcolm.

Ellen O'Leary cried, "Oh, Colin! Have you seen this before?"

XXI

I'm sorry, Nooky," said her brother jerkily. "It happened—long enough after we came—so that I felt—it wouldn't happen to us. I hoped you wouldn't know. There are so many things—that we can't help."

"We got to try," said Red McDougal. "I can't stand it. Never could."

He was already striding down the slope that faced the vanished lake. Colin O'Leary, stumbling alongside, panted, "I did try. He was—nearly dead, but I got him out. I couldn't make him understand me, though. I had to let him go. And they—put him back. He was dead when I—"

They reached the field of sunken grasses, tried to cut across it; but the mud mired them deep. They struggled out and took the longer way, skirting the jungle. J. G. Hall thought apprehensively of poisoned darts.

Malcolm McDougal, younger than his father, longer of leg than Colin O'Leary, reached the man first. The stones were ponderous and very old; the sunlight, slanting on them, lined the worn symbol of the hawk god. But the mystery of centuries was nothing, for that tortured head was human and alive. Two heavy slabs prisoned the neck, the lifted arms, even the shoulders; and the face was toward the lake. The man was meant to die, not rapidly, of thirst—with the lake before him.

Only of thirst. The feet were on the ground; the head could move a little. Malcolm saw the bloodshot eyes turn toward him, without wonder, without hope.

And memory was back across a dozen, fifteen years. Malcolm McDougal saw the wide, green, smiling country of the Marañon. A river rolling in the bush, a wide, great river where the traffic of the world should come. His father, that serene and mighty man, sure of his destiny, luck riding at his shoulder in those days. An Indian sidling from the bush, afraid, but fascinated by a thing he didn't understand—a great, red-bearded white man peering through a transit.

Long ago, Malcolm McDougal heard his own voice piping, "Daddy, look! He's got two noses!"

But the slabs were very heavy. Heaving, Malcolm grunted to O'Leary, "How the hell did you ever do it by yourself?" Then Red McDougal put his gaunt strength to it, and the stone went down; and Malcolm caught the Indian as he fell.

Joan Hall was civilized, but she didn't even notice that the man was completely naked. She had heard of split-nosed Indians, but that wasn't the shocking thing. The man appeared to have two noses, single-barreled, but it didn't seem a mutilation; only a deformity. The awful thing was the way the tongue protruded from the tortured mouth.

The man was making tortured sounds: "*'Mpá'. 'Mpá'.*"

Umpás. Water. Red McDougal lifted the Indian in his arms and plowed into the mud. His gaunt weight pushed his boots deep into the mud; he floundered and fell headlong with the Indian. Malcolm ran to help him—tried to run—and saw the Indian turn his face into the mud, trying to suck a little moisture. But the water was a long way off across the mud.

"Can't make it, Red. We'll have to carry him to camp."

The Indian wasn't much to carry. He was skin and bones, an old one. Malcolm carried him to land and plodded off around the mud. But pity made him hurry; he began to pant, and Red McDougal said, "Here, kid. I'll carry him awhile."

"Let me," said Colin O'Leary.

"H'mph!" said Red McDougal to the slender man.

Colin O'Leary was humiliated, Joan could see. She took his wiry, slender arm and walked with him.

Malcolm ran on ahead and clambered down on the broken dam and filled his hat with water. Over the noise of water, then, he heard the shouts of men, like the howls of animals. They'd seen him. They came running along the ledge. They were pretty dusty, and the howls were broken, coughing. Malcolm grinned and galloped back with the water.

Colin O'Leary saw the dusty men, and his heart smote him. They had breathed a lot of the poisoned stuff; they must have stirred it up like madmen. Colin O'Leary hoped they hadn't damaged his priceless mummies.

Harvey didn't know quite what to make of what he saw—the muddy men, the muddy, naked Indian. Coughing, he said, "What's this?"

"Find anything?" said Malcolm.

Harvey was no tenderfoot. He knew what was the matter with that Indian. Thirst—in sight of all that water!

"I don't get it," said Slick Harvey.

"Stick around," said Malcolm, "and you will. We all may. Just because you don't see any Indians, that's no sign."

Slick Harvey knew it was no sign. He knew what things could happen in the jungle; and a chill came over the hot sunshine.

One of his men said, "What's the matter with his tongue?"

"He got that way," snarled Harvey, "talking too much."

Fearful, the man said, "Indians?"

"Wha'd'ye think?" snarled Harvey. "Eskimos?"

His eyes were red. That was the way it came—the sickness of the poisoned dust. A chill, then fever. Colin O'Leary said, "Better get back to camp. You're going to be pretty sick."

"How would you like to go to hell?" snarled Harvey.

And they went in silence down the split of Iscacinga. Their human minds peopled the hot stillness of the cliffs, peopled the noise of water with the sound of creeping feet. They had, for the moment, little thought of gold.

O'Leary's hut was cooler than the tents. Old Red McDougal laid the Indian on O'Leary's cot and gave him a little water and a little whisky, and a little water at a time. The tortured gasping deepened to a tortured croak.

Old Red McDougal answered gravely, "*Mana.* No."

And Joan saw the hopeless eyes and cried, "Why do they do it? I don't see how human beings can!"

The big man answered heavily, "You got to make allowances. They're ignorant. They're superstitious."

"What has superstition got to do with torturing a poor old man like that?"

"I got a notion," said the big man, "it's the old ones mostly that get tortured. He keeps askin' if his son's come back. And I remember—"

In his grave and heavy voice he told them of that split-nosed Indian on the Marañon, far to the north. A young one, wearing on his smooth brown chest an amulet of—slag, the refuse of an ancient smelting.

"I was pretty sure he came from Iscacinga. But I didn't know where Iscacinga was. Not then. I tried him in the Pana dialect, and Ucayali; and he understood a little. Must have learned it after he left here. This man talks Keshua.

"And he admitted it, but he was scared. He said a thing I couldn't figure then. He said, 'I am an orphan!'

"Well, I've got a kind of a notion now. It must be the young ones mostly that run off. . . . This was a sacred place. A secret place. That's why they branded 'em—to keep 'em from runnin' off. You couldn't hide a thing like a split nose. Whoever saw you, anywhere, would know you came from Iscacinga. That's what Iscacinga means. . . . But a man could hide a long time in the jungle. So they figured out this way to make 'em come back of their own accord.

"It must be hard to keep on runnin' when you know they got your papa trussed up like a turkey, dyin' by inches, every minute that you're gone."

"Then this man's son—" said Joan.

"Well, I don't know. We'll ask him, soon as he can talk."

"You think he'll tell you?" said O'Leary.

"I don't know," said Red McDougal, his blue gaze averted. There were things you couldn't explain to white men.

Indians called all white men *viracocha,* lord. That was no more than white men did: "mister" meant master, and *señor* meant lord. But Red McDougal knew that Indians, jungle Indians, had a superstitious awe of him. It didn't make him proud; it made him humble. He knew why. It was because of his great stature, his red hair and beard. In the dim centuries that no man knew, in the dim legends of a race whose glory had gone out in darkness like the sundown of the tropics, there had been a bearded man, a god whose name was Viracocha.

Red McDougal didn't say, and Malcolm had forgotten, how that Indian on the Marañon had cried in superstitious fear, "I am without a father. . . . He is dead, lord. Do not punish him!"

XXII

TOWARD sundown, though, the Indian woke and stretched a withered hand to Red McDougal, croaking, "Mercy, lord!"

The big man said uncertainly, "*Samani.* Rest."

"What did he say?" said Joan.

The big man mumbled, "Says, 'have mercy.' Out of his head, I reckon."

"Did you notice what he called you?" said O'Leary.

"Yeah," said the big man, mumbling. "That's what they call every white man—*viracocha.*"

"Yes, but he doesn't look at us. He looks at you."

"Because I'm bigger. Easier to see."

"I wonder!" said O'Leary.

"Wonder what?" said Red McDougal, truculent, embarrassed.

"If he doesn't think you're Viracocha."

"Who?" said J. G. Hall.

"One of their gods. The one that corresponds to our own Christ. The one who taught them how to live. A bearded man. A white man!"

"Rats!" growled Red McDougal.

"Why?" said Colin O'Leary, and his quiet eyes were glowing. "In the Maya country, too, they have the legend of the bearded men. What gave them the conception? Indians don't have beards. And there's the theory that all the Incas—all the ruling caste—were white. The Spaniards tell us they were bigger, lighter-colored than the subject races."

"Yeah," said Red McDougal. "They had more to eat, and didn't have to work out in the sun."

"That doesn't explain the beards. And it doesn't explain so great a difference in size. When Atahuallpa offered ransom to Pizarro—offered to fill a room with gold as high as he could reach—they marked it on the wall. And do you know how high that Inca reached? Nine feet!"

"I know," said Red McDougal. "Must have been a freak. I couldn't reach that high myself."

"There isn't any evidence that Atahuallpa was a freak. Incas were big. They were another race; that's known. They spoke another language. And they tried to keep the race from breeding out. They married their own sisters. But the men had concubines; that's why the empire was already dying. Atahuallpa was a halfbreed; that's established. I believe— That's why I'm here," said Colin O'Leary, and his quiet hand took in the land behind the Andes. "I believe that white men came along the Amazon, four thousand or twelve thousand years ago."

"From where?" said J. G. Hall.

"Atlantis, maybe," said the slender man.

But Red McDougal didn't know there had been such a continent. The mystery of sunken land, of lost millenniums, was past, was gone; tomorrow was still coming. And the tortured Indian watched him with submissive, trusting eyes.

"Your son has run away?"

"Yes, lord."

"What is the law?"

Stoic, the tortured eyes went shut. The Indian answered faintly, "I am ready, lord."

The big man sat in silence for a moment, while the muscles worked across his cheek bones under his grizzled beard. He said without presumption, "Have no fear, my son. The law is the law no more."

Old Red McDougal, who had no religion, had a superstition of his own. He called it luck. It was a power greater than the hills, and greater than the strength of men who bucked the hills and tried to tame the jungle for the use of men.

It helped you, and the jungle opened, and the hills lay down before your human brain. It turned against you, and your strength was nothing. But you couldn't quit. It gave you dreams. It favored men who had the guts to try.

The sun swung down on Iscacinga, and the Indian didn't know it swung across an ocean where the ships of men went sailing between cities. But old Red McDougal knew. He tramped outside and said to Charley Farr, "Look, Charley. How's the dynamite? Got any left?"

"About a dozen sticks. That dam took quite a shot."

"Two sticks is plenty. How do you feel?"

"Oh, pretty good. Say, what do you reckon's in that dust? It makes you sicker'n a dog. But it wears off."

"I hope it don't wear off too soon," said Red McDougal, "far's Slick Harvey and his roughnecks are concerned. We got a ticklish job to do, and I can't get along with Indians if I have to keep apologizin' about white men."

"Goin to finish breakin' down the dam?" cried Charley, hopeful.

"No, and we better hope it don't break down itself. We got to wait. But if those Indians once find out we're human—"

Dawn swept up again on Iscacinga, and the big man went to Harvey's camp and said, "Look, Slick. How do you feel?"

"Rotten," said Slick, or bitter words to that effect.

"That's good," said Red McDougal. "Do you want to take my word that I ain't after the *peje grande?* Not today. I'm huntin' Indians. Tryin' to make friends. We got to, or we'll be in trouble from now on. You reckon you can keep your roughnecks quiet?"

Harvey spoke with scorn of Indians. Being civilized, he never said quite what he meant.

The Indian, old and sick, could travel slowly. They went slowly up the split of Iscacinga, into the fertile valley where the lake had been. They came to that awful pillory of stone. The Indian, trembling, looked at Red McDougal, but his thin old legs still held him up.

The big man said, "Be not afraid."

You had to try. Old Red McDougal didn't know just why he bared his grizzled head before he roared into the silence of old centuries, "*Jamuni!* Come."

Nobody came. The bush was silent in the sunlight, in the stillness of dead centuries. Colin O'Leary said, "I doubt if they can hear this far. Their village is a mile away, where the lake empties—used to empty."

"Keep your shirt on," said old Red McDougal, listening. "I don't want 'em to come too soon; and if I didn't tell 'em to, they might."

He nodded to Charley Farr. The little man got down by one of the thick pillars where so many men had died, and the clink of steel was sharp on an age of stone. The drill bit cleanly under the blows of steel. One hole was finished, and the little man began on the other one. There was no other sound that anybody else could hear; but Red McDougal stiffened.

"Come!"

The stirring in the jungle stopped, not near enough for danger yet—not near enough for deadly bits of fluff, for wooden spears in that dense vegetation. But the holes were finished, loaded, and nobody came.

"All primed?"

"Uh-huh," said Charley Farr, and showed the yellow bits of dynamite in the split fuses, that would burn more quickly, surely than the fuses.

"How much time?"

"Two minutes."

"Light 'em. . . . Come along. Get out of range. Don't hurry."

They moved off into the stillness, and the ticking of his watch was loud—a big watch, but a tiny thing to measure heavy seconds to the crashing of a door between the dead past and the living future.

"Stand away. The law is the law no longer. Viracocha speaks."

Erect and gaunt, old Red McDougal faced the sun, the ancient stones between him and the sun. Twin threads of smoke were curling there. Tick-tick, tick-tick. He lifted up his hand. A sharp, clean crack of dynamite went racing off into the hills. Another followed. Colin O'Leary groaned. The timeless pillars had dissolved in smoke.

The deep voice rolled on the stunned silence of old centuries: "My children, come!"

They came. The bushes stirred in the sunlight. One by one they slipped into the sunlight, brown, half-naked creatures; and their faces bore the ancient mutilation, and their eyes had the ancient fear. The men gripped weapons, wooden clubs and spears and short, crude blowguns, but they made no gesture. And the split-nosed women came, the children after them, naked as they were born. The adults, past the age of puberty, wore strips of crudely woven cloth. Colin O'Leary, watching in strange detachment, knew that all the ancient art was dead. The law could live without the animating brain.

The weight of superstition, the inheritance of humble generations and the law of men long dead, was on them. Even the babies had split noses—cut through cartilage and bone, kept open, not allowed to heal. Joan Hall was a little sick.

The deep voice rolled again into the silence: "You are free. The law is the law no more."

Their eyes were black, uncomprehending. Red McDougal knew it had to be more definite for them. He laid his big hand on the shoulder of the man beside him, the sick, trembling old one, saying slowly, "This one, first that Viracocha pardons, shall be honored. You are free, and your sons are free. The law is the law no more."

He turned his back and slowly walked away. The others had the wit to match his pace, his bearing, holding their backs against the fear of flying death.

It didn't come. They dared look back, and saw the Indians melting into the jungle. Malcolm murmured, "Wha'd'ye think, Red?"

"I don't know," said Red McDougal wearily. "You got to give 'em time. But I had to try it. Couldn't let 'em truss that poor old feller up again if I could help it."

"What did you tell 'em?" demanded Joan.

"Told 'em they had a right to run away. I hope they will. They haven't got a chance to keep white men from comin' after gold. Not now. Even if we—" He stopped. You couldn't say things like that to women. This was no place for women, but they'd better take a chance with Indians than some white men.

XXIII

GOING down the split of Iscacinga, Charley Farr dropped back unnoticed and was glad to be alone. He wanted time to comprehend this thing. No harm in that. Slick Harvey and his roughnecks were in camp. The Indians were back yonder in the jungle. Charley was not afraid of Indians. He had never learned their language—any of their languages; but all you had to do was treat them halfway decent, and they let you pretty much alone.

Charley was used to being pretty much alone. White men confused him, talking all the time.

He laid his horny, freckled hands against the cliff. A hill of gold! He knew it, but it didn't look like gold or feel like gold. Machinery and time must intervene before it felt like gold. Charley was nearly seventy. He had no thought of dying; he had lived with timeless hills so long that he was timeless to himself. But he was old and tired with following a dream, and lately it had blazed before him—gold, gold of the Incas, mined and smelted long ago, forever smooth and rich and heavy to the hands.

The *peje grande!* Where? The little man stood gazing at the unknown walls, the fallen stones of the drowned tower. Water was all about them yet. But maybe in the channel, where the scouring current ran, the mud would be less deep. Maybe a man could reach them, walking in the water.

He climbed down on the broken dam. The stones were loose, the water rushing through them. Incas had had no mortar; they had had no lime; and they had lacked the skill, or patience, of that older, unknown race before them, who had built the mighty walls that stood forever without mortar. This was an Inca dam, plastered with clay and banked with earth; and once the water flowed across it, it was gone.

A stone turned under him. He didn't mind wet boots, but he did mind a broken leg; and that was easy at his age. He scrambled wildly for his balance. But he fell. His boots plunged into water, and his arms plunged into water and struck stone. Hurt, panting, Charley Farr lay on his face, propped on his aching elbows, and the sliding water was an inch from his startled nose.

The shadow of his head obscured the sun. And in the shadow, in the rushing water, was a glint of gold.

The little man moved slowly, not because he knew that he was hurt. He sat up slowly on the stones and plucked the nugget from the water. It was gold. It wasn't a big nugget; not much bigger than a pea. But it was gold. And it had come out of that wide, flat valley, out of that mud where men could not yet walk. The water had washed it down. The tumbled stones had caught it, like a sluice.

How many others? Charley Farr got up, and didn't know that he was hurt. He splashed on the broken dam.

He tugged at stones. He could lift some of them, turn some of them and let the water roll them down. He found another nugget, a mere grain of gold, caught in a narrow crevice. Even his hard hands were torn, but he didn't know it.

He ran up and got his drill to pry at stones he couldn't move. He didn't know that he was tearing down the dam.

Exhausted, Charley Farr stood up in the water, and some sanity returned to him. He knew that he was old, and hurt, and a little dizzy. But the gold was real. He fished the nuggets from his pocket and caressed them. They were real, and they had come out of that valley where the lake had been.

The water was strangely lower. At its edge was a line of red between the water and the mud of rotted vegetation. Red! And black sand drifted in the water, sharp against the red. Black sand, red clay! The little man plunged in his hands, cupped, barely submerged in the current, and the black sand settled in them. Slowly; he had to tilt his hands when he lifted them, to let the sunlight strike. The sun was strangely low.

The voice of Red McDougal spoke through the noise of water: "What are you doin', Charley?"

"Huh?" said the little man, not really hearing. For the sinking sun struck tiny glints of its own metal in the drained sand. It was all here. Black sand, red clay— and a hill of gold. A dream, a nightmare, too much gold for any man to comprehend. The little man stood up and babbled vaguely, "Gold. It's gold. It's gold, Red."

"You don't say," said Red McDougal heavily. "And how much good will it do us if those roughnecks find it out?"

"But look. This sand. That clay. This is another *infernil*—fifty times bigger than the *infernil*. A cinch to work. You know the clay of the *infernil?* Stribnite, pyrite, sulphide of antimony—no sulphur. Iron and tourmaline and gold. Free gold, I tell you!" Charley Farr threw down the sand and pawed his pockets. "Look!"

But he had thrown the nuggets with the sand. He threw himself into the water, clawing at the water. Red McDougal had to scramble down and haul him out of it, sobbing.

"Nuggets. I had 'em, Red. I swear it."

"Sure," said the big man. "I believe you. We've got hold of somethin' just too big to handle. But we've got to try. We've got two women with us; and if this thing busts—I'm just as crazy as you are. But I'm tryin' not to be. Try, Charley. Come on back to camp. Whatever's here won't get away, unless we give it away."

They went on back to camp, and Charley knew that he was old and dazed and hurt; and that was all. Gold, for the moment, had become a nightmare, nothing fit for human comprehension. Night banged down on Iscacinga, not a time for rest. They talked in whispers, conscious of Harvey's men in the camp above them. J. G. Hall, who dealt in millions, all his life had dealt with symbols merely; he had seldom touched the metal of the sun. He felt the fever, stranger than the sickness of the poisoned dust.

He whispered, "This will mean a new gold standard for the world. The world needs gold. Nobody ever dreamed of so much gold in one deposit."

"No," said Red McDougal. "We're all dreamin', and we'll all go crazy if we don't look out. I never dreamed I'd get two women into such a fix."

"Can't we just stake our claims and get away?"

"Slick Harvey ain't exactly dumb. He knows that people don't go stakin' claims unless they're claimin' somethin'. And those fellers he's got with him—they ain't oil men. I been fooled about Slick Harvey. He came here all fixed for trouble. He knows what we're after. I'll be fair with you: I'm scared to make a move. I'd hate to have those fellers crazy too."

"Seven of us, and six of them," said J. G. Hall.

"You're crazy," growled the big man. "Seven, yes—if you count two women! And we got one pistol and one shotgun, and those fellers have got everything but cannons—and they're used to usin' 'em. Haven't you seen their eyes?"

"That isn't what I mean," said J. G. Hall. "Why not just tell them? Let them stake claims too. Thirteen," said the man of millions, thoughtful in the starlight, groping for sanity in purple darkness; and he tried to be facetious, smiling in the darkness. "Thirteen claims. Unlucky number, but— How much can one claim cover in this country?"

"In this country," said the big man, and his hand took in the lonely darkness, "all that you can grab, unless somebody gets away to talk about it."

And the man of millions understood at last that there were no policemen and no lawyers at his call; that millions, in this lonely land, could only drive men crazy.

"What shall we do, then?"

"I don't know," said Red McDougal. "Maybe we can wait 'em out. Or maybe I can make Slick Harvey think I had a hunch that worked out wrong. A wild-goose chase. Then we could get away. I doubt it," said the big man heavily. "I'm not much good at lyin'. My one chance is to keep my mouth shut, mostly."

Red McDougal was himself again, the Red McDougal of these later years, uncertain, fumbling. J. G. Hall was silent. Charley Farr sat silent in the starlight, dazed, his bruised and battered hands between his aching knees. The gold was here, and there was nothing he could do about it.

XXIV

IN THE brushwood hut, by the light of a lantern, Malcolm and Joan and the O'Learys played at contract bridge. It wasn't easy to begin, but Colin O'Leary kept them at it, saying, "Nothing is the hardest thing in the world to do."

And they were civilized, accustomed to the use of symbols. None of them saw past the printed shapes—the hearts that stood for hot intrigues; the diamonds that stood for riches; clubs that were tamed to symbols, spades that had once been swords. The contest was just a game. But Malcolm, his nerves on edge, fired into it the truculence, the hard, red-headed hate he would have vented on Slick Harvey and his gang. He played with savage energy, disastrous energy.

He said, "I'm goin' to quit readin' stories. In a story, we'd sneak up and murder 'em tonight, and then get married and live happy ever after."

Joan, aggressive too, said sharply, "If you'd read a book or two between your stories, you might know what bidding means. Or even if you'd read your hand before you bid."

"That's a swell crack," said Malcolm savagely, "from you. Haven't you heard? They've repealed the law against passing. You don't have to bid, this year, unless you've got a card or two."

"Haven't you ever heard of distribution?" said Joan Hall.

"I have. But aces still take tricks, most of the time."

Ellen O'Leary laughed and said, "You just don't hold together."

"Oh, we hold enough," said Joan. "But cards don't bid themselves, or play themselves."

"Or sike themselves!" said Malcolm.

"Maybe that's it," said Ellen. "Maybe you're both too psychic. Colin and I are both too timid. . . . Play with me, Mac, won't you? Might make two good teams."

Colin O'Leary, smiling, said to Joan, "You'll have to be patient with me. I'm inclined to be absent-minded."

But he wasn't. He was merely quiet. When he bid, Joan knew he had 'em. There were no more jarring sets. The game grew tight, absorbing; it beguiled their minds into the channels used by generations. They forgot Slick Harvey and his gang. The cards, the symbols, swung the play, and they felt civilized again.

They came to the morning rested, these four young ones. J. G. Hall, the business man too far from lawyers and policemen, was uncertain, troubled and withdrawn. Old Red McDougal, the responsible, was silent. Charley Farr, his spindling bones one solid ache, his solitary mind confused, cooked breakfast without knowing what he cooked. Malcolm McDougal tried to cheer the little man.

He grinned and said, "Well, Charley, what are you goin' to buy with your four tons of gold?"

Charley said shakily, "We got to git it first."

The sky was cool and blue; the shadow of the peak was opalescent, and the men who moved in Harvey's camp were merely men. Malcolm McDougal was unable to believe in real disaster. Trouble always passed. You fought it off, or laughed it off. He grinned, suggesting, "How about a thousand grand pianos? And a fleet of automobiles? And a flock of English butlers? And a—"

"Git away from me!" squalled Charley.

"Don't," said Joan to Malcolm, whispering. And Joan was fresh and crisp and lovely in the morning; Malcolm realized that he was young and strong and rested, that it wasn't fair to bait an old man, a tired little man.

Malcolm said soberly, "Don't worry, Charley. We'll come through. We're not dead yet."

"Maybe," said Charley shakily, "we just don't know it yet."

Malcolm McDougal was ashamed. He didn't know just what to do about it. Malcolm McDougal hadn't often been ashamed.

Colin O'Leary came and asked old Red McDougal, "Have you decided what we'd better do?"

"No," said the big man heavily.

"Will it be all right if I go on working? All this sort of thing is new to me, and I'm used to working."

"New to all of us," said Red McDougal. And he

grinned with strangeness, rising to gloomy flippancy. "I doubt if anybody's used to findin' so much gold they don't know what to do about it."

J. G. Hall suggested, "Can't we all pretend an interest in archæology? It might make Harvey think—"

"It won't," said Red McDougal. "Harvey knows how long I been around this country, and he knows I ain't no guide. But if O'Leary don't mind havin' us around, it's better than just doin' nothin'."

So they went again into the split of Iscacinga. Harvey and his men came sauntering, only a little wabbly from the dust, facetious and intrusive; but it wasn't easy to believe that there was danger. Harvey, seeing them tie handkerchiefs about their mouths and noses, said reproachfully, "You might have suggested that to us."

"I did," said Colin O'Leary, and believed it.

"Told you it would make you sick," said Red McDougal.

But nobody went into the tunnel. Colin O'Leary only went on working on the mummy he had been unwrapping when this strange invasion came. His skillful, quiet hands took off the yards and yards of gorgeous fabric, woven before the Spaniards came, before there had been such a race as the one now called American. They crowded the open chamber where the ancient dust came thinly—restless, these Americans; and only one of them was busy, and there were two women of the breed.

At the base of the squatting mummy, in the ancient basket, were the things he had taken with him into the timeless dark—three earthen pots, glossy and black and shaped with art into the portraits of expressive human heads; and there were bits of greenish gold, shawl pins and nameless trinkets; and the death mask of thin gold was on the floor. But Harvey, gauging the amount of gold, was not excited.

It was Joan who suddenly was that. She bent and snatched one of the priceless pots and smashed it on the ear of a man named Mike, a swarthy man whose bold, affectionate black eyes were hardly Irish.

Mike said, "*Porca madonna!*" and grappled with her.

Malcolm said in literal translation, though not wittingly, "You swine!" and smacked Mike on the jaw, which was quite open, as Mike's hands were otherwise engaged. Mike's arms relaxed, and Mike slid slowly down Joan Hall and slowly toppled toward the edge of the rock; but Malcolm caught him as he slid toward thirty feet of empty space. Malcolm was civilized.

Malcolm said hotly to Slick Harvey, "Tell your rats to keep their dirty—"

"Rats?" said a man named Al, a lashless man whose eyes looked scalded and whose face was peeling with raw sunburn; and his voice was smooth with the habit of a place where men feared irony because all men disguised their true intentions always—civilized. "Did you say rats?"

There was a smooth black automatic in his hand. Malcolm McDougal looked at Harvey, grinning, and said, "Lay 'em on the table, Slick. What's the idea? The way

I get it, you're an oil man. You've been ridin' on Red's trail for years, because you think there's oil on the Marañon. Well, that's all right, if you believe it. But what license have you got to bring a bunch of hoodlums in here when we—"

"Hoodlums?" said the man named Al.

"Shut up," said Harvey, smiling. "Put it away, Al. Mike had it coming to him. Put it away! I'll tell you when."

They were all civilized. Colin O'Leary went on working with his trembling hands, his quiet, earnest brain that was so used to searching in the unknown past that it could hardly grapple with the helpless and fantastic present. Colin O'Leary was an archæologist, and he was used to quiet, used to working thoughtfully, carefully, prayerfully, probing with gentle hands and gentle brain into the places no man knew. Pushing the bounds of human knowledge into the past. Malcolm McDougal, engineer, son of old Red McDougal, engineer, thought only of the future. J. G. Hall, the business man too far from lawyers and policeman, watched his daughter; and he blamed himself that he had brought her here—from safety, from the luxury and safety that his toil could give her—just because he was so tired of things he knew so well. The child had never been so lovely, so desirable as now, when eyes profaned her. Joan was brave, and J. G. Hall was proud. Ellen O'Leary, thin and hard, was much less lovely. Both the girls were dressed like men, and Ellen O'Leary might have been one. Little and thin and hard, a pencil in her hand, she was taking notes of what her brother did; she seemed to have no thought of masculinity, of danger.

It was Red McDougal who said suddenly, "Where's Charley?"

Charley Farr was bored. He would have shot the man named Mike if Malcolm hadn't hit him; but the thing blew over, and the man O'Leary went on working on the useless mummy, tickled to find a *tupu,* shawl pin, with perhaps five dollars' worth of gold. The little man no longer thought in dollars' worth of gold. He thought in pounds, *arrobas,* tons. And it was here. If you lived long enough to get it.

And the minutes and the hours were slipping by. The little man stood restless on the ledge of rock outside the open chamber in the rock. Nobody noticed him.

He went along the ledge and down the stairway in the rock. He went back to the broken dam where he had found the virgin gold, and lost it.

Surely there was no harm in that. Nobody ever noticed Charley Farr, and all he wanted was to stand and look.

But when he came in sight of the dam, he saw that the way to the unknown walls, the fallen tower in the lake, was open. Now the strip of red between the water and the black, the mud of rotted vegetation, had grown wide; the walls were nearly free of water; and the clay, the red clay—stribnite, pyrite, iron and tourmaline and gold—was hard. He walked upon it easily. He reached the walls. But they were empty. And to him it didn't matter, but he knew why water hadn't pushed them down when the lake emptied. They were built of stones so closely cut as to need no mortar—built before the Inca dynasty began.

But the tower, built with stones less great, had fallen in the moving water. That was Inca. That was built in the period when men had hid the gold.

He waded in the water, on the hard, firm clay—stribnite and tourmaline and gold. He climbed on the tumbled stones. A *huaca*—house of the dead. But what protruded from the stones, at his very feet, was not a mummy.

It was gold. It wasn't black with time; there was no sulphur in this water—no free sulphur. It was merely green. He tugged it free. It was a vessel, wide and flat, its use too vague for Charley Farr. It weighed perhaps twenty-five pounds. He laid it on the stones and scrambled down into the water and brought up a handful of black sand and scrubbed it across the vessel. It was gold.

The little man began to heave at the tumbled stones. They were not big stones, and they were not squarely cut. They rolled. Almost at once he came on another thing of gold, an edge of thicker gold, not easy to uncover. It went down too deep.

He tugged and panted at the stones, and he forgot that he was old and tired and little. He had found the *peje grande*—big fish, gold of the Incas, more than the

Spanish fleets had carried off to Spain, gold that the Incas carried off and hid to keep it from the Spaniards. What the Spaniards got was the little fish, the old men said. The Incas, that strange, canny race whose rule had reached from the Argentine to Panama, had hid more gold than all the Spaniards ever found. Millions and millions of it. Back to the gods that gave it, and no man knew where but Charley Farr.

The little man stood up and panted, but the stones still held the golden vessel fast. The scratches of the stones were deep in its soft green surface, yellow and soft and rich. He tried to guess the size of it by symmetry. He tried to guess the value of it. What could he do with so much gold?

"A thousand grand pianos. And a fleet of automobiles. And a flock of English butlers. And a—"

Charley's heart was pounding, and his mind refused to work. He ought to be imagining great happiness, but he was only tired. He knew that he was nearly seventy. What could he do? Why had he hunted it so long—this yellow metal, useless in itself? What could it buy him that he really wanted? He was nearly seventy, and he had been content for fifty years, hunting for gold—content with just a little vein or two.

The little man stood up on the tumbled stones and panted, staring at the thing—that huge and senseless piece of metal, green, with yellow scratches in it.

"Ah!" said the man named Al.

The little man turned dimly. Dimly he could see the man named Al. But it didn't mean much. Gold was only metal, after all these years.

"Hello," said Charley Farr.

"What's this?" said the man named Al. "Found something?"

He climbed up on the tumbled stones and peered at the great vessel buried in the stone. He touched the yellow scratches.

"Gold!" said the man named Al.

"I think so," said the little man.

"So this is what McDougal came for!"

"Huh?" said Charley Farr.

And suddenly his brain began to work again. No matter what this thing was worth, it belonged to Red, to Malcolm—Mac, whom he remembered as a baby. Mac was a flip kid, and a nuisance sometimes, but old Charley Farr was fond of him. And J. G. Hall, the tenderfoot who had put up the money. And his daughter, that slim gal who had the guts to stand a trip like this. And young O'Leary and his sister, who had found it first, who had already been here, even if they didn't know just where they were.

"You get away from here!" squalled Charley Farr.

"Oh, yeah?" said the man named Al.

"You heard me," said the little man.

On the same instant their two hands began to move. But Charley Farr's big black revolver, worn from years of resting in its holster, not from use, was frankly at his hip, on the path his hand must travel; the man named Al, who lived in cities, who was used to drawing unobserved, had to reach to his left armpit. Charley beat him to the draw.

The man named Al withdrew his hand and grinned and said, "Don't shoot. I'm on my way."

"You better be," said Charley Farr.

"Oh, yeah?" said the man named Al.

For Charley Farr incautiously had dropped the muzzle, trusting, unaccustomed to such men as Al. And Al's left hand slammed down on the gun, and Al's right fist crashed home on Charley's jaw. The little man went down on the tumbled stones. The man named Al stood over him, with Charley's own gun in his hand, and pulled the trigger.

Nothing happened. Snap! And that was all. The old man, struggling up, had time to thank his lucky stars that he had been too full of the thought of gold to change the cartridges last night, after their wetting. Charley Farr began to grin, to speak, but the only human voice that spoke was the voice of the man named Al. And that was only a contemptuous word as the man named Al threw down the useless gun and took out his own automatic, never wet, never neglected.

Red McDougal, in the chamber of the mummies, said, "What's that?"

It sounded like the far-off, rapid back fire of an automobile. Charley Farr had gone to a place where streets were gold and there was never any spending.

XXV

THE man named Al was not accustomed to the exercise of his profession in broad daylight, in the open, in a place where men could see so far. He wasn't used to so much sunlight. He was used to crowded and electric-lighted streets where many people moved, where many automobiles moved, where you could cruise unnoticed till you saw your man open and unprotected—on the spot; where, stepping on the gas, racing away after your man was down, you threw the traffic into confusion and cut off pursuit. No peaceful citizen could think or move as fast as you could. Peaceful citizens were hindered by the fear of law.

The man named Al was not afraid of law; only of men. His habit was to shoot and get away. His mind was trained to speed in that respect. But how could you make speed without an automobile, in the middle of a wide, flat valley filled with mud and sunlight?

Loud and unmistakable, to Al, the echoes bounced from the split mountain where the men were; and there was no other way to run except along the stream, where they could see him for a mile. Charley was very dead, and Al was trapped there with the evidence. Before the echoes came across the valley from the farther hills, Al had begun to act by habit, dragging the little man down out of sight behind the stones. Hiding behind the fallen tower, Al took off his hat and watched between the stones.

The sound of the shots came faintly into the split of Iscacinga, drowned by the noise of water and confused by cliffs, without direction. Red McDougal said again, "Where's Charley?"

Malcolm heard it too. Slick Harvey's men were lounging on the ledge outside the chamber, taking no chances with the poisoned dust; but one was missing. Malcolm said, "And where's the guy that pulled his gun on me?"

Slick Harvey smiled behind his dusty handkerchief. He hadn't heard the shots. He murmured, "Better leave well enough alone, Mac. I don't know Al very well, but I doubt if it would pay to push him into a corner."

"Any rat," said Malcolm grimly. "Wha'd'ye mean, don't know him well? Who brought him here?"

"Oh, I did. But he comes well recommended, I assure you. He's a friend of Mike's. . . . Eh, Mike?"

The man named Mike, his swarthy skull still throbbing, glared and said, "Well, what about it? Deesa guy want some trouble?"

"Never mind," said Harvey. "It's not time yet, Mike. We haven't found the gold."

"What gold?" said Malcolm, hard, red-headed, mocking.

"Never mind," said Harvey, mocking too. "You wouldn't know. You came along just for the ride. Or maybe," said the smooth man, cutting his eyes at Joan, "the company."

Joan hadn't heard the shots. The safest place for her and Ellen was inside the dusty chamber, where the roughnecks didn't want to come. No sense of strangeness rode her, standing in the silent rock, inside a cliff of gold, with men all masked like burglars; she was only glad her own mask hid her trembling mouth. Joan Hall was not a tourist now. She was a woman and afraid.

They had to get along with Harvey if they could. She hoped her eyes were mirthful, crinkling at Slick Harvey. She was glad to hear her voice come clear, light, flippant, quite as it had been in Lima, in a city, at a softly lighted dinner table—civilized.

"You flatter me," said Joan. "Mac and his father are an excellent pair of guides, but I assure you they don't take a pair of tourists just for the company. They get the money. Ask my father!"

J. G. Hall said dryly, steadily, "I'm not complaining. Glad to get 'em. But let's get this straight: You still believe we're hunting gold?"

"Why, no!" said Harvey. "All you want is solitude. Just solitude!"

"Exactly," said the man of millions, and his voice had sharpened uncontrollably. "Is that too much to ask?"

"Oh, much too much!" said Harvey. "Even if Mac and Red don't care for charming company, I do."

Old Red McDougal went along the ledge till he could see the broken dam, but Charley wasn't there. He moved a little farther, and he saw the ruins; and he knew a man could reach them now. The water, stripping the mud, had shrunk; that clay, conglomerate, was hard enough to walk on.

"Charley!"

The deep-lunged bellow faded in the sun. Nobody answered. Charley wasn't there.

Old Red McDougal didn't dare climb down and look for footprints in the clay, attract attention to the ruins. Maybe the shots had come from camp, in the other direction. He went back and said to Harvey, "Come along. I'm goin' to look for Charley—and your friend the gunman."

"Sure," said Harvey, idle and complacent.

Colin O'Leary tried to go on working with his mummies. And Joan Hall blamed Malcolm for his foolish truculence, blamed Colin for his cowardly, inhuman calm.

XXVI

THE man named Al saw Red McDougal come out of the split and glance into the valley, shouting Charley's name. But Charley lay quite harmless, staring at the sun. The man named Al began to breathe more easily. What was he worrying about? McDougal was the man Harvey was after. Harvey would be glad to know that one of McDougal's men was gone, wiped out. And Harvey would be glad to know—

The gold!

The man named Al lay motionless. The unfamiliar sun, that could be torture to an unaccustomed skin, swung slowly overhead; but Al endured it, motionless. The heat and brightness of an unfamiliar thought were burning in his brain.

He was used to money. In the United States, in years just fading, murder was well paid. But not in gold. The man named Al could read. In the United States, in hiding, reading to pass the time away—reading the papers that so kindly warned you that the dicks were on your trail—the man named Al had learned that gold was more than money. It was against the law to have it. Money was going down, but gold was going up. Not his to reason why; he only knew that gold was more than money. Gold was gold, a flaming thought, a fever.

And this heap of stone, smelling with strangeness in the nostrils of a city man, was full of gold.

He didn't mind the smell of blood. He had rarely smelled it; mostly he got away too fast. He didn't mind the thought of death, so long as it wasn't his. There wasn't much blood anyway. Al knew his business—knew that the surest way to stop a man was to shoot him, quickly and often, in the stomach. It was self-defense—Al easily believed. The little guy would certainly have killed him for the gold.

That was the trouble. Harvey, who was after gold, would want to know what it was all about.

Calculating angles, keeping the stones between him and the split of Iscacinga, Al dragged Charley down into the water. Carefully he piled a dozen stones on top of Charley, taking care that none of them should rise above the water. Watching the split of Iscacinga, ready to duck if he saw any movement there, he wriggled up to see if any blood was on the stones. He lugged the stained ones down and dropped them in the water. He rolled stones again around the great green vessel Charley had been trying to uncover, hiding it. He took the smaller vessel with him. He could hide that somewhere else.

It was a token. It consoled him, waiting for that blazing sun to drop—the burning eye of heaven. Not that Al feared heaven. What he feared was men, covetous men who might demand an explanation of the thing he carried—a mere twenty pounds of gold.

The man named Al was not himself, enduring heat

and light. The sudden sundown of the tropics jarred him into motion. But before he reached the split of Iscacinga, suddenly, he saw electric torches moving there. He turned and ran, clutching the precious vessel. Passing the ruins, trying to round the water, for a little while he floundered in the mud; but he got back to the firm clay along the water's edge beyond. The starlight showed him the red path of safety. Looking back, he saw the torches stop where he had stopped, and then come on. He turned and ran into the unknown darkness.

Red McDougal said, "They came this way. And neither one came back."

"Look here," said Malcolm, pointing with his torch. "Al came this far. And turned around and went back. Running!"

"How does it happen," said Slick Harvey, "that there aren't any other tracks? Haven't the rest of you been out to see these ruins?"

"No," said Red McDougal stolidly. He had no heart for subterfuge; not now. He said, "This was a lake. We started draining it two days ago. The water's been too high until today."

The big man cursed himself that he had waited. Charley was a solitary man, he knew; and Charley was no tenderfoot. Charley was used to traveling his own trail. Surely, old Red had argued, Charley would show up by sundown. But he hadn't—and the man named Al was missing too.

Slick Harvey wasn't worried. Charley was no friend of his, and Al was just a thug. Harvey was civilized, no thug; he was a business man. But things did happen in the hills, and oil was where you found it. So was gold. You didn't have to make reports on everything you knew—so long as you got the oil. And if you got the gold—enough gold—you could tell 'em all to go to hell. Chiefly the man was curious about those ruins in that wide, flat, starlit valley, where no living man had been except these missing ones.

The massive walls were empty, Harvey saw. But Red McDougal plowed directly to a heap of stones in the water and announced, "Charley was here. Charley had hobnails in his boots." He swung his modern flash light all about, and saw no other sign of Charley. But the stones at a certain place had been disturbed, less dried than others by the sun.

Then Malcolm, scouting along the water's edge beyond, said, "Here you are. This is the way he went."

"Who?" said old Red McDougal.

"Al," said Malcolm grimly, scouting on.

The tracks were spaced, the tracks of a man running, but not regular; the clay was slippery, and more than once the man named Al had fallen. Once or twice the clay, where his hands had struck, bore a strange imprint, but nobody stopped to study it. The water swung away into the south, shrunken again into the bed that it had followed centuries ago; but they were not concerned with ancient water. Modern torches, swinging in the timeless dark, showed where a pair of modern boots had left the clay and plowed into the mud.

If Al could pass it, so could they. The mud was narrow here, and stone rose under it. Old Red grunted, "Village around here somewhere."

"How do you know?" said Harvey.

"Spillway, this was—where the lake emptied. This is where O'Leary says they live. Be careful."

But there were no lights in the jungle. They went slowly down the bed of a drained stream; the trail of muddy boots ran on. The torches swung and showed the jungle crowding.

"Wait. I hear 'em."

"Who?" said Harvey.

"Walk behind me. Slow," said Red McDougal.

XXVII

THE man named Al had gained a quarter of an hour while they poked about the ruins. Looking back, he saw them stop, and he didn't wait to see if they came on. He had to get around them and get back to camp. He had his story ready—lost in the jungle, trying to get back to camp. He didn't believe a man could really get lost this close to camp. Not Al. He knew that split-nosed peak, and here a gully turned in the right direction, with a good, firm, gravel bed. His boots were loud on the damp gravel.

Something whistled past his ear and whacked into the creek bank and stood quivering. A wooden spear. Al whirled about and stared into the darkness, afraid to move, afraid to turn his back. His hand, mechanical, grabbed for his automatic. It was gone. He'd dropped it, one of the times that he had fallen. But he hadn't dropped the golden bowl.

He tried to speak but couldn't. Silent shapes were closing on him in the darkness. Indians! Then his voice came, begging hoarsely, "Get away! Friend! *Kamerad! Amigo!*"

Silently they closed, those dim, brown, naked shapes. They didn't touch him; but the man remembered. He had seen one of their victims. Indians took a fiendish pleasure in slow torture. Dimly, in the starlight, he could see their faces, horrible, inhuman, with two noses each. They walled him in the darkness, cutting off escape, but they didn't touch him. They came just so far, and stopped—and let him suffer.

That was because the Indians didn't know just what to do. This man was one of those the great one called his brothers; and the great one said the law was not the law. . . . The man named Al, unable to endure their silence, struck a match.

Their voices cried in wonder at the miracle of instant fire. They shrank away from instant fire—these superstitious men who had forgotten how to build a fire, who only kept it through the centuries. They never had the need to build new fire. They were not nomads; they were prisoned here, cut off from all their kind, keeping the law whose givers they no longer knew, the will of kings long dead. The gods. Their faces bore the sacred mark of Iscacinga—giver of gold, the metal men no longer used, the lost, forbidden metal of the sun.

The man named Al, not understanding, was a little reassured. But the match went out, and he could hear their voices in the dark, not human, not in syllables that he could understand; in syllables too harsh and guttural for human speech. He tried to strike another match. But his hands fumbled, and he had to hold that heavy bowl under his elbow.

Then he remembered. Gold! Enough to buy the whole tribe, the whole countryside. Even a pack of savages must know the worth of gold. The match flared, and he offered them the bowl, croaking, "It's gold." His life was precious to the man; and gold was precious, but he knew where there was plenty more.

He saw their faces change, and that was all. Something had struck his arm. The match went out; he dropped the bowl, but he didn't know it. He was fighting for his life, kicking and striking in the darkness, even biting. And he screamed for help, but even he could hardly hear his hoarse and muffled voice. The taste and smell of human bodies overwhelmed him, dragged him. He could feel the jungle clawing, and the stars were blotted out. He plunged against a wall of brushwood, and the hands released him, but he found no egress. A dim, slow-burning fire was on the floor. The hut was full of shadows and dim, horrible, inhuman faces—with two noses each.

A thin, inhuman voice was speaking, not in human words. The man named Al was limp, numb, paralyzed. He watched the fire. How soon? He knew what could be done just with a match, held lightly at the soles of the bare feet. But Al had never tried it on himself.

A light showed in the darkness, dim, rectangular. A door! But he couldn't reach it. Hands fell on him, accurate, and dragged him down. These animals could see in darkness!

Then a deep and quiet voice was speaking somewhere, in the guttural, explosive syllables the Indians used; but it was not the voice of an Indian. Al tried twice before he found his own voice screaming, "Hey, McDougal! Help!"

"Hold everything," said Red McDougal. "Even if you're hurt, don't show it. Keep your mouth shut and be quiet."

Al was quiet, but he couldn't keep his mouth shut. Blinding light came through the door, a dim, huge figure stooping after it. The figure moved into the middle of the hut, the only place inside the hut where Red McDougal could stand upright; and he didn't seem to know that one of his boots was almost in the fire. The flash light swung about that circle of inhuman, split-nosed faces, of black, blinded eyes. The deep voice spoke. The cracked one answered, stammering. The deep one spoke again, slowly and long, but dimly to the man named Al.

The flash light swung and pointed at the door. Brown, naked shapes got up and moved into the fan of light, moved out into the darkness.

"Get up on your feet," said Red McDougal. "Slow. Walk out behind me. Slow."

The slow and heavy movement of the bearded man restrained Al's frantic need to run, to dash into the darkness. Then he heard the casual, smooth voice of Harvey in the darkness.

"You all right, Al?"

"Sure," said Al, gasping.

"They didn't hurt you?"

"Naw!" said Al. For modern flash lights showed him

where to put his feet, and he saw no split-nosed Indians; he was suddenly alive and safe.

"Sorry to hear it," said the young McDougal. "What did you do with Charley?"

"Who?" said the man named Al, sparring for time. It came to him that they didn't know or they wouldn't be asking. "Oh," said Al, "you mean that little freckled guy?" Then he remembered another detail, somehow vivid. Charley's hat had fallen off, and Charley was entirely bald. Al wondered for a frantic second whether he'd remembered to sink Charley's hat. He had. To prove it to himself, he added, "Bald?"

Too vivid. Al was not himself; it seemed a long, inhuman time before the young McDougal said impassively, "Yes, bald."

Al cried, "I haven't seen him!"

"When?" said Harvey smoothly.

"Wha'd'ye mean?" cried Al.

"I'm asking," said Slick Harvey.

"Well, I'm telling you! I haven't seen him!"

"Then don't shout," said Harvey, murmuring. "We're not exactly deaf. Nor dumb."

"You mean," cried Al, "I am?"

"I fear," said Harvey, murmuring, "you are. I'm sorry I took Mike's word for you. Mike said that you were regular."

"You mean I ain't?" cried Al. "You wouldn't say that if I had a gun!"

"No gun?" said Harvey. "I've been wondering about that. I didn't see any dead Indians—and a coward always shoots. What did you do with it?"

"Lost it! Fell down in the mud and lost it. Lost it, I tell you!"

"While you're telling us," said Harvey, murmuring, "suppose you tell us what inspired you to go promenading in the mud. Into the jungle. After sundown. You!"

"Got lost. Went out to see the ruins, and got turned around. Just trying to get back to camp!"

Then Red McDougal spoke, the first time since they'd left the Indian village, and the last time till they reached their camps on the lower slope of Iscacinga. Gravely and contemptuously, he said, "That's possible, I reckon, for a city thug. But we'll find out tomorrow."

And they went along the margin of the vanished lake, between the jungle and the mud; and Al was not himself. The silence let his thoughts go flying off into the dark. Indians were in the jungle, and tomorrow was out yonder in the mud.

The stars wheeled slowly over Iscacinga; and he wasn't used to things that happened slowly. He was used to speed, to quickness, to confusion that diverted human minds from what was really happening.

He went with Harvey to their camp above the brushwood hut. Before they reached the camp, though, Harvey stopped and murmured, "Spill it, fellow."

"What?" said Al. "Spill what?"

But Harvey only stood and waited. Harvey wasn't big

or noisy or impressive, and he made no threats; but he could wait. And so could Indians. And the stars were wheeling slowly toward tomorrow, and a man was helpless if he had no friends.

"All right. I killed him."

Harvey stood and waited, cold as any snake. Al had to say it all; and it was easy, once he started talking. Gold! It warmed this vast and strange and lonely darkness. He was not alone. Harvey was with him now. Harvey was smiling; Al could see his teeth. Al spoke in confidence. He said, "I'm on the level, see? I didn't have to let you in. But you're the boss."

"You double-crossing so-and-so," said Harvey, smiling.

XXVIII

CHARLEY didn't come. Old Red McDougal knew he wouldn't come. Charley was out there somewhere near the ruins. Maybe in the ruins; maybe under those turned stones of the fallen tower. Maybe in the water. Red McDougal hoped he was in the water—that stout-hearted, plodding little man, come weary to the end of a long seeking. In the water he could lie out flat and rest.

Colin O'Leary said, "Maybe some Indian saw what happened. I believe they watch us all the time."

"Yeah, likely. But I couldn't let 'em tell me."

"Why?"

"Because we're white men. Got to let 'em think that we can manage our own business. If they get the idea that we're human—"

"H'm!" said J. G. Hall. "How are you going to keep them from it? We're not all as big and picturesque as you are; and white men are going to swarm here, from now on."

"I know," said Red McDougal heavily. "That's what I mean. They think no human's got a right to come here, and we got to give 'em time to realize. Get used to it. If they start fightin' us, they'll get the worst of it, of course; but they'll kill white men, too. And what's the use?"

"Why haven't they killed me?" said Colin O'Leary.

Red McDougal lifted his somber gaze from his muddy boots. He tried to say a thing he knew, not easy to explain to white men. "Maybe," he said, "because you didn't expect 'em to."

Malcolm McDougal sat in grim and bitter silence. Malcolm knew the breed of Harvey's men, a modern breed, born of the jungle of the law, the tangle of too many laws. The tangle might be straightened out, too late for Charley. Fifty years the little man had moved in safety in the hills, among the Indians, in a land not tamed by men; but a rat had killed him.

Malcolm couldn't sleep. When he heard a sound from Harvey's camp, he thought of Joan and Ellen. When he shut his eyes, he saw the trail of Charley's unreturning boots—lopsided, worn with many trails, tramping through golden clay to a timeless tower. . . . Only the man named Al had come away. A rat, a modern, driven from the cities to this quiet land behind the hills.

The starlight drifted through the canvas of the tent where Malcolm tried to sleep. It had no fly, no outer roof of canvas; this was not the rainy season. Charley had known his business. Even on a trip with a man of millions, Charley hadn't brought a pound of needless weight. . . . You needed tents for privacy. There was a woman in the party. Civilized . . . He heard the quiet breathing of his father and Joan's father. Charley used to snore, but Charley's cot was empty.

Malcolm sat up slowly in the darkness and pulled on

his boots. He took his flash light, but he didn't turn it on. He took Red's shotgun and slipped out and listened at Joan's tent till he was sure he heard her breathing. Then he started climbing toward the split of Iscacinga.

"Where you goin', kid?" said Red McDougal.

"I can't sleep," said Malcolm.

"Neither can I. But there's no use goin' off half cocked."

"I've got to know," said Malcolm.

"Don't you?" said his father.

"Yes. What are we going to do about it?"

"Nothin', yet. Sit down, kid, anyway. I want to talk to you."

They sat on stones not carved by men, and Iscacinga loomed under the stars. Some old convulsion of the earth had squeezed it up, had concentrated here more gold than men had often found in hills of earth, before there were such things as men. And men had come here long ago to pluck what gold they could with tools of stone. It wasn't money then. It was the metal of the sun. The gods. Those men were ancient in the scale of human time; yet they were new against the scale of earth, brief in the eons of the spinning planet—men, born of the earth but reaching for the stars.

These moderns didn't think of that. The young one thought of Charley Farr; the old one thought of Charley and a thousand, many men like Charley.

"Look," said Red McDougal. "In the first place, kid, we got two women with us. In the second place, the way we act right now will have a lot to do with how the Indians take what's comin'. And it's bound to come. This country's goin' to be settled up."

"So what?" said Malcolm bitterly. "With white men?"

"Yeah. And I don't mean we're any better than the Indians. But it's white men do most of the settlin', kid, you can't deny."

"Like Al?" said Malcolm.

"No. You got to make allowances for men like that."

"You—what?" said Malcolm.

"Keep your shirt on, kid. I'll get that feller, or die tryin', if we prove it. But I'll get him by the law."

"The law!" said Malcolm.

"Yeah."

The stars wheeled slowly on that land behind the Andes, and the young man thought of yesterday, tomorrow; but the old one saw the years behind him and the years to come.

"You can't remember, kid. When I first saw the valley of the Marañon, I— Maybe I can't explain. Just beggin' to be settled. White men think the tropics are just terrible, but they forget there's such a thing as altitude. They think Peru is dry because they haven't crossed the Andes. I admit the Andes are a lot of hills, but when I saw that country, I just knew there had to be a way to reach it. And I found the way."

"I know," said Malcolm.

"Yeah," said Red McDougal, "but you're young. I mean—I don't know how to tell you what I mean. The

Marañon ain't far away. Not when they once start comin' after gold. I mean— Look, kid. If anything happens to me, will you go on and build that railroad?"

"Hell!" said Malcolm. "Red, don't be a fool!"

"I ain't, kid. But I'm gettin' old. And anything might happen in a fix like this."

"It has," said Malcolm grimly. "They've got Charley, and they may get us tomorrow. Come on back to bed."

He didn't really believe it. He was young. He knew that Red was getting old, of course; Malcolm was old enough to grasp that simple fact. But Red was Red. He was a fixture, like the Andes, like the Marañon. Charley was different. Charley, to Malcolm, had been always old. A little man, a funny little man. A man; and a rat had killed him.

It was nearly dawn before the young man went to sleep. What woke him was the sound of his father dressing in the dark.

"What's up?"

"They are," said Red, whispering. "Be quiet. Don't wake Hall."

"You can't," said J. G. Hall. "I'm awake already."

"Well, go back to sleep."

The tents of Harvey's men were glowing in the dark. The man of millions said, "What's up?"

"Nothin', for you. I want you to stay here."

"Is Joan—"

"So far. That's why."

"You tell me what to do," said the man of millions, "and I'll do it."

"For a tenderfoot," said Red McDougal, "you're a wonder."

Malcolm began to dress. The big man said, "No, kid. You stay here too."

"Says you!" said Malcolm. "Think I'll let you take those hoodlums by yourself?"

"Do what I tell you," said his father gravely. "I ain't goin' to take 'em. I'm just goin' with 'em."

"Where?"

"Only one thing liable to get those fellers up this time of day. Al must have told 'em somethin'. Maybe what Charley found, and why he shot him. Listen, kid. You tell O'Leary and his sister to stay home today."

"I'm going with you."

"No, you ain't. You're liable to lose your temper and get shot. This ain't no funny business—not if Charley found what I think he found."

"And you," said Malcolm, "can't be shot!"

"Well, I don't aim to be. It ain't so easy, kid, to shoot a man that can keep his temper. But you can't. Not yet. You're young."

"Before I'm older," said the hard young man, "I'll have one try at squaring things for Charley."

"See?" said his father gravely. "Get me killed, and get yourself killed, and leave just two men—and Joan and Ellen. You stay here."

Malcolm and J. G. Hall stood watching that huge, patient figure climb in the light of fading stars. They saw the smaller figure of Slick Harvey step out of his tent to meet him, and saw Harvey's men come out and cluster about him. Malcolm was half dressed, Red's shotgun in his hand. But nothing happened. Joan came out in her pajamas, and her clear young face was pale and drawn with sleeplessness, but she was lovely. Malcolm hurled her back into her tent.

The sun burst up on Iscacinga, bland and sweet, uncaring that such tiny things as men were crazed by its yellow metal.

XXIX

Ellen O'Leary had been wakeful too. Ellen was used to lonely places, used to following her brother, used to the dull and peaceful labors of an archæologist. All this was strange, unreal—the feel of evil. It was strange to Colin too. But Malcolm came, dynamic, vital, used to action; and his eyes were sober, but his hard mouth grinned.

"Red wants you to stay in today. Will you?"

"What are you going to do?"

"Twiddle my thumbs," said Malcolm ruefully. "As Colin says, the hardest thing in the world—just nothing."

"Let's play bridge," said Ellen.

"Oke," said Malcolm carelessly. He stood in the doorway, watching her cook breakfast; and his eyes were calm.

"You're swell," said Ellen, "for the nerves."

"Who, me?" said Malcolm. "If you take me on, gal, you'll find out. Only the jitters could persuade me to play bridge at half-past six in the morning."

But he grinned. That was the thing. His father was with those gangsters, but he grinned. Ellen O'Leary grinned and went on cooking breakfast.

That was a strange game, not well played. Colin O'Leary, used to concentration, made no bad mistakes; but even he was using only half his mind. The other half had gone with Red McDougal, climbing the split of Iscacinga, going out into the upper valley where the lake had been. To the unknown ruins. What was there? The body of the little freckled man, he was convinced. And danger for Red McDougal, Malcolm's father. And what else? The gold—not money, but the wrought gold, record of a vanished empire. Running how far back? Four thousand or twelve thousand years; astronomers could not agree. Twelve thousand years ago a continent had almost spanned the broad Atlantic. That way white men might have come.

Colin O'Leary played with half his mind, but Malcolm played with less. Malcolm McDougal threw into the game the flippancy that was his one defense against reality. He knew what Red was up against, and there was nothing he could do about it. Red had told him to stay here.

"Five spades," said Malcolm, "and jump out the window."

"Double!" said Joan, exasperated, sitting behind him with three aces and the king of spades.

Ellen O'Leary, thin and hard and weather-beaten, smiled and said, "Redouble."

Then Joan knew that she was hooked. The hand must be a freak; Ellen was void in both red suits. Joan had suspected it. She cried, "Six diamonds!"

"Double," said Ellen, smiling.

And she wasn't void in either hearts or diamonds. Joan, down three, cried angrily, "You had your nerve!"

"Thank you," said Ellen, smiling. "Mac was the one who had the nerve. You had the cards he hoped I had."

"Maybe," flared Joan, "I'd better hold my hand up!"

Colin O'Leary said abstractedly, "You don't mean that."

"Don't I!" said Joan.

"Do you?" said Colin, gentle and distressed.

"Of course I don't!" said Joan. "Colin, don't be a fool!"

"At bridge," said Colin, "I'm afraid I am."

"You're not!" cried Joan Hall, furious. "I am. Let's quit!"

"Suits me," said Malcolm, shrugging.

"I should think it would!" cried Joan.

"Okay!" said Malcolm.

And the angry ones got up and left the brushwood hut. Joan, trembling—whether with anger or with fear, she didn't know—accused him, "You deliberately spoiled the game!"

Malcolm said wearily, "I'm no fit company for man or beast. I can't stop wondering what's happening up yonder."

Then she knew that it was fear. She cried, "Neither can I. Let's go and see!"

But Malcolm hesitated, strangely spineless; and it made her more afraid. Her father, sitting quiet in the sunlight, said, "Sit steady, youngsters. Red knows what he's doing."

"Just the best he can," said Malcolm, "but—"

"I wonder if he does!" cried Joan.

Malcolm McDougal shrugged and said, "I guess nobody does."

"And you admit it!" cried Joan Hall. "You won't stand up for your own father!"

"Steady," said J. G. Hall, but Joan paid no attention. Malcolm sat down on a rock and started tossing pebbles at the stream that brought no word of what was happening.

The older man went tactfully inside the men's tent. J. G. Hall could manage men and millions, and himself, but not his daughter.

Strangely, to herself, Joan Hall began to cry. Malcolm said glumly, "Don't, Joan. That won't help."

He reached a hard brown hand and drew her to a seat beside him; and he said, "Hold everything. Don't worry, Joan; Red knows his way around."

"It makes me—so afraid when you're afraid."

He petted her. He said, "I'm not afraid," and added with a grin, "exactly. I'm just petrified." That was so far beyond the truth that he himself was comforted; and suddenly he knew the truth. He said, "Trouble with me, I'm temperamental. I can't stand suspense. Don't worry; Red's all right. He knows his way around."

And Joan believed it now. Malcolm was strong; he knew this strange and lonely land behind the hills. Joan Hall was comforted. She said, "I'm temperamental too, I guess. Thanks, Mac. Forgive me."

"You?" said Malcolm, and his voice was rough, but

his eyes were tender; and Joan smiled. The sun was growing hot, but neither of them felt it. Malcolm kissed her, gently, and then not so gently. They forgot the anguish of suspense.

Ellen O'Leary's low, surprising voice said suddenly, "That's rather foolish, don't you think?"

They saw her in the sunlight, thin, impersonal, embarrassed; and they knew that she was right. Malcolm McDougal cast a startled glance at Iscacinga, was relieved to see nobody coming through the split. He said, "Of course it is. . . . I'm sorry, Joan."

"Are you!" said Joan, for she, too, saw that they were unobserved except by Ellen—by that thin, hard, sexless creature who dared look at her with scorn. At her, Joan Hall! Joan found relief in anger. Smiling, she said icily to Ellen, "Would you like my seat?"

A dull, slow wave of red rose from the open throat of Ellen's mannish shirt, flushing her thin, hard cheeks. Her gray eyes steadied and her voice was quiet, saying, "Sorry, Joan. I don't mean foolish. I mean risky."

And she turned away. But Joan flew after her and caught her arm and cried, "Ellen, I don't know what I'm saying!"

Ellen said wearily, "Who does, today?"

XXX

THE man named Al, walking behind Slick Harvey and the big McDougal into the upper valley, saw the evidence against him; saw the prints of Charley's boots lead to the ruins, saw his own prints over them sometimes. Carefully, unobtrusively, he walked exactly in them now, grinding his feet to blur that unreturning trail. He had to grind his feet; the clay was drying on the surface.

"Notice what Al's doin'," said the big man, though he hadn't looked.

Slick Harvey turned, expressionless. Al stopped. You never knew how Harvey would take anything. But Harvey turned away, and Al went on obliterating Charley's trail.

They came to the ruins, and Al splashed at once into the water, to the fallen tower. Climbing on the stones, he said, "Right here," and started lifting stones and throwing them into the water—choosing the lighter stones and throwing them well out into the water, at the spot where he had piled the stones on top of Charley; and the glancing sun hid what was there. Al came at once to that buried rim of gold, and the other crowded up and started clawing at the stones. Behind them, Al began to look for something he'd forgotten yesterday.

Unnoticed, he was sure, he found it—Charley's gun.

He tossed it in the water, and the splash was covered by the splash of stones. The big McDougal didn't seem to notice; only stood there in the sunlight, huge and motionless, his beard sunk on his chest. The man named Al climbed up and threw more stones than anybody.

Red McDougal threw no stones. His somber eyes were fixed on the spot where they were digging, but he knew already. Charley wasn't there. He knew where Charley was. But he had to wait. You couldn't stop a bunch of roughnecks with their hands on gold.

The stones were flying, rolling, tumbling; and the great green vessel came to light, incredible unless you knew such things existed. Part of old Red McDougal's mind was far away, in Lima, in an almost modern city, in the cool and quiet office of Don Carlos A. Romero, scholarly director of the National Library of Peru. His gaunt old nose could feel the half-moon glasses that he used for reading, and his sun-bleached eyes saw ancient words that he deciphered to forget his own frustration.

"Gold of XXI carats. . . . Vessel which weighed fifty-eight pounds eight ounces, which are one hundred and seventeen marks. . . . Vessel which weighed twenty-seven pounds. . . . The figure of an Indian. . . . Drums of gold. . . . Fountains of gold. . . . The figure of a female Indian. . . . Plates of gold . . . pounds . . . pounds —"

Ounces and marks and pounds and tons of gold the Spaniards looted, listed like merchandise and shipped to Spain. The lists were long, but what the Spaniards got was the little fish, the old men said. This was the great one, treasure of temples that were empty when the robbers found them. Sacred vessels, sacred emblems, plates of the glowing metal stripped from the temples of a dying empire and sent back to Iscacinga—back to the gods that gave the gold.

But that had no significance to Harvey's men. Before the stones released the great green vessel, voices had begun to shout at other finds. The man named Mike, the swarthy one whose eyes were hardly Irish, cried, "*Madonna!*" and caught up a small green statue of a human figure, female, draped; and it was queerly like the figure of a Virgin white men knew. But that was not its value to the man named Mike. It weighed perhaps two pounds, and it was gold.

He didn't waste much time on just two pounds of gold. He stuffed it hastily in his hip pocket and helped tug the heavy vessel free. It weighed perhaps two hundred pounds, but it didn't stop them.

Nothing stopped them but fatigue, sheer animal exhaustion. Vessels and plates of gold, figures and shapes of gold, battered with stones and green with the slime of centuries, lay piled with increasing carelessness before they stopped; and they were down to the water, but the gold went deeper. Red McDougal understood. This tower that had crumbled was a symbol merely. It had borne the shape of a *huaca*, house of the dead; but Inca masonry could not sustain a *huaca* big enough to hold the treasure of an empire. Most of the gold was underground.

These men were never hardened to the toil of stones; and it was hot. The sun whose stronghold they profaned was past the zenith, but they didn't know it. They were dazed. They tried to comprehend it. Gold—that heap of slimy metal; for the stones made rich and yellow scratches in it, and their hands had felt its weight, its texture. But they couldn't feel its value. There was too much gold.

They had to rest. Then Red McDougal moved. He clambered slowly down into the water.

"What the hell?" cried the man named Al, dizzy with heat and toil, remembering.

"You wouldn't know?" said Red McDougal, plowing on.

He stooped and groped in the water and found Charley, and with gentle hands he lifted off the stones. He lifted Charley in his arms. Nobody was surprised. They only wondered what he meant to do about it; and what could he do? He plodded back, not climbing the stones again, but stumbling around them on the landward side, heading for camp.

They followed. They were tired and dizzy, and they had to eat. Only the man named Al demanded, "What about it?"

"You tell me," said Red McDougal, plodding. "Did you have some notion you could get that gold all by yourself?"

Slick Harvey smiled. Al cried, "It was self-defense, and I can prove it!"

Al ran back and fished up Charley's gun. He didn't know just how to work it; he was used to more modern weapons. But he found the way. You had to lift a dingus and push out the bulky cartridges one at a time. He showed their bases; two of them were dented.

"See? His gun missed fire, that's all!"

"I see," said Red McDougal. "But who pulled the trigger?"

"Huh?" said Al.

"You ran away last night when you saw us comin'. You hid Charley in the water, and you wiped out Charley's tracks this mornin', and you threw that gun in the water—your one proof that it was self-defense."

But Al was still without a gun. Slick Harvey said contemptuously, "You dumb gorilla! Do you think this is Chicago or New York?"

And Al, misunderstanding, breathed more easily. You didn't have to beat the laws out here. There weren't any.

Only for a moment. Smiling, cold as any snake, Slick Harvey said, "Don't look for me to save your skin. There aren't many white men in this country, and they're spotted every minute. Everybody knows which way they went; and if they don't come back—"

Al whispered, "What if none of 'em come back? We haven't seen 'em, see?"

The man named Mike lifted his brows inquiringly. But Harvey was a realist, and he saw all the picture; and he wasn't ready for six murders, yet. Including women.

Harvey was a realist, and he had not yet realized. He

was an oil man; that was too much gold. A hard game, oil. The man named Mike, the man named George, and the two others—Nick and Finney—worked for Slick Harvey's company, under Slick Harvey's personal direction; but they did it at a distance, not while Harvey was along.

It wasn't easy to shoot a man in the back, or even to see it done, if you'd never done it.

Red McDougal, a romantic, saw more clearly. Men were fumbling, yearning animals, with visions greater than their minds could grasp. He knew Slick Harvey, and he knew Slick's vision—all the oil there was, regardless; but Slick needed time to change his mind to gold. And Slick had been his enemy for years, yet they were somehow friends. Slick wouldn't shoot him in the back. Not yet. Old Red McDougal had no time to be afraid, with Charley in his arms—little old Charley, dreaming gold for fifty years, and spared the need to wonder what his gold could buy.

Old Red McDougal was an animal; he'd get the man named Al. But he was human, civilized. He'd get him by the law.

He carried Charley to the brushwood hut. He made no effort to spare Joan and Ellen the sight of Charley; they already knew. He said to Malcolm, "Get the pick and shovel, kid." They buried Charley by the halfbreed wrangler, Juan. But this was different, and not because the little man was white. Juan was a sacrifice to ancient gods, but Charley was a sacrifice to gold.

Slick Harvey and his men were animals; they had to eat. They stayed away from Charley's funeral. They couldn't stay away from gold, though. Harvey came and said, "What's on your mind, Red?"

"How do you mean?" said Red McDougal.

Harvey had begun to realize; his eyes were restless and his voice was sharp. He said, "I wouldn't advise you to go running off in the heat of the day without a blanket."

Red McDougal answered stolidly. "We won't, Slick. We'll be here when you get back."

XXXI

Colin O'Leary was an animal, afraid, not only for himself; but he was human, too—an archæologist. His anguish wasn't all of fear. Clutching his sister's hand, he begged of Red McDougal, "Are they damaging the artifacts?"

The big man said untruthfully, "Not much." They were. The gold was rich and soft, and they were wrenching it by force from the grip of stones. Old Red McDougal lied to keep O'Leary from a foolish risk. He knew the passion of an archæologist.

The unseen condor of the gods drew down the flaming symbol of the gods, and the black puma, night, pounced on the world; and Harvey and his men came back. They were a little drunk with weariness and gold. And they proceeded to get drunk with something else, as Red McDougal knew they would. Men had to celebrate. When thoughts had spurred their hearts into fatigue, they had to spur their hearts to give the thoughts reality again. Then they would think of something else. With pounding pulses, they would think of what could make their pulses pound.

Hilarious and loud the voices came. Then Malcolm stiffened. Colin O'Leary stiffened. J. G. Hall looked apprehensively at Red McDougal. Voices were coming down the hill, and they were arguing first choice of women. That was Joan. Ellen O'Leary, white and quiet, moved to draw the curtains; but old Red McDougal shook his head and said, "No use. That'll just make 'em think we're scared."

Ellen O'Leary had to grin. She said, "What are we?" Red McDougal had to grin, admitting, "Scared. But let's pretend we're peevish."

And before the voices came, he stepped outside and loosened his deep and quiet voice into the darkness: "Slick!"

"Wot ho?" said Slick, himself a little drunk.

"Come here a minute."

But three other men came first—the man named Mike, the man named Nick, the man named Finney. Red McDougal said, "Good evenin', boys. Find lots of gold?"

But they had found too much gold, gold beyond the limits of their comprehension. Women were not beyond their comprehension—not with their pulses pounding. The man named Mike said, "Hell wit' you! Get out of t'e way."

"Says who?" said Malcolm, in the door, Red's shotgun pointing at Mike's stomach.

"Keep your shirt on, kid," said Red McDougal; and his voice was calm, but a shotgun pointing at the stomach was a calming factor too. The man named Nick, leaning against the brushwood wall, could feel it give, and was inspired to push; but the shotgun swung, and Nick stopped pushing. Mike and Nick and Finney all had guns, but they were undecided—yet.

Slick Harvey came and said, "What's on your mind?"

"These fellows," said old Red McDougal. "Tell 'em to get away."

Slick Harvey said indulgently, "Be reasonable, boys." Slick Harvey, drunk with weariness and gold and something else, was still a business man, still civilized; the thing that still could make his pulses pound was gold. He wasn't afraid of Red McDougal—yet. And Mike and Nick and Finney were not ready yet to kill for women.

Red McDougal said, "Come in, Slick, and sit down. Let's talk this over. I'm as fond of gold as you are, but I've got two women on my hands."

"I don't believe," said Harvey, smiling dizzily, "I can persuade my boys to let you have a cut."

Colin O'Leary said, "A cut? You think you're going to divide that gold among you?"

"I don't see why not. Do you?"

"They're artifacts. Under the law, archæological finds belong to the government. You can't get ancient artifacts out of the country."

"Who'll prevent us? You?"

"The government. Back here behind the hills, you might be able to get 'em into Bolivia or Ecuador, or even Colombia; but it won't do you any good. They've got the same law as Peru. You can't ship ancient artifacts."

"They won't be artifacts," said Harvey, smiling, "when we ship 'em. Does that ease your mind?"

"You mean," O'Leary cried in agony, "you'd melt 'em down?"

But Red McDougal threw him a grave and quiet glance and said, "Of course. . . . The point is, Slick, what about us?" And Harvey, for the moment, found no word to answer. Harvey didn't know. The big man said again, "I've got two women on my hands. What can you guarantee?"

And J. G. Hall, accustomed to the use of power, tried to use it now. He said, "Remember, Harvey. Mahon's a friend of mine."

Then Harvey laughed, a little dizzily, and said, "So what?"

"He's chairman of the board," said J. G. Hall. But even as he spoke, his voice had weakened. The directors of Consolidated Oil were powerful—in oil; their arms were long enough to reach around the world—in oil. But why should Harvey care for oil if he had tons of gold? The man of millions knew his voice had weakened. Gold, the measure of all business, could make business nothing.

Harvey laughed. But Red McDougal said impassively, "Stick to the point, Slick. What about us?"

"I'll do my best," said Harvey lightly, dizzily.

And silence fell, in which the voices came from the camp above. The deep and quiet voice of Red McDougal broke it, saying, "Well, you'd better, Slick."

"How come?" said Harvey, smiling. "Getting rough?"

"I'm tellin' you. And I advise you to remember."

"Yeah?" said Harvey, smiling.

Red McDougal answered nothing. Nothing at all. He only sat there, huge and massive and apparently a little bored. The celebrating voices came from the camp above. Slick Harvey, smiling, said, "I fancy you'll excuse me?"

"Gladly," said J. G. Hall.

"Remember," said old Red McDougal.

And the stars swung, and the voices died in weariness, in stupor. Red McDougal said to Red McDougal's son, "We got to beat 'em to it, kid. You come outside. I want to talk to you."

They sat in the purple darkness by the stream, on the very rock where Malcolm had sat with Joan; but the young man had no time to think of that. His father came abruptly to the point. The young man cried, "You, Red? You wouldn't do a thing like that!" The song of water covered that startled protest—water, running swift and changeless down the valley. Westward lay Peru, the Urubamba and the Ucayali and the highlands of a vanished empire; northward the mighty Amazon, the wide, green, smiling country of the Marañon; eastward, the way the dawn would come behind the split-nosed peak, Brazil, the dark Chaco, never tamed by men. But water, swift and changeless, bearing grains of gold, was running again into the channels where it had not run for centuries.

No time? The deep and quiet voice went on, spreading the land before young Malcolm's eyes; spreading the reach of time old Red McDougal could remember and the reach of time his blue and vital eyes could see ahead. It disengaged young Malcolm's mind from the troubled present, made him see it as a moving point in a panorama.

"Time," said old Red McDougal, "is the one thing we got to work with, kid. The question is, can you keep your temper?"

"Yeah," said Malcolm soberly. "Whether I can or not, Red, you can bank on that. I will."

XXXII

THE first place Harvey looked, in the early dawn, was at the horses. Horses couldn't walk on tiptoe; he was pretty sure he would have heard them if they'd tried to slip away in the night, except that he had been a little drunk. He had slept more heavily than usual; but he was pretty sure old Red wouldn't be fool enough to try to slip away. You couldn't get far in the dark—not in this country, with two women and a tenderfoot like J. G. Hall. You could be overtaken, easily, before you reached the Urubamba.

The horses were all there. Not all together; Harvey wasn't fool enough to take a chance with his own horses; they were tethered close to camp. Let anybody try to steal 'em! In this country, horses were important. You were pretty helpless if you had to match your human legs against these distances.

And smoke was rising from the brushwood hut, and smoke was rising from the camp below. Malcolm was cooking breakfast. Harvey could see him. Harvey wasn't hungry, but he wanted coffee. He went in and waked the man named George.

Harvey had time to think while George was making coffee. Gold! His heartbeat lifted. Tons of gold, there must be, if you got it all. You couldn't realize it, but you knew. Slick Harvey sat in a sort of daze. Unconsciously, he watched the camps below—O'Leary's hut; O'Leary was an archæologist, and said you couldn't get away with ancient artifacts; and Red McDougal was a massive, patient man—no fighter, but tenacious. Harvey, sipping coffee, was unconsciously considering.

But there was time. They couldn't get away.

The man named Mike came out. The sun was up; the shadow of the peak was opalescent, cool and sweet. The man named Mike gazed hungrily at Red McDougal's camp. Joan Hall was moving there, slender and graceful in her white, beautifully tailored breeches, not like any man. Mike grunted, "Quite a gal, huh, Meester Harvey?"

"Quite," said Harvey; and by habit he spoke coolly, but the land was vast and empty, and the sun flamed, and the thought of gold was a thought of power. Harvey added, "Don't get optimistic, Mike. I may discuss that with you."

Ellen O'Leary stepped outside the hut. Mike grinned and said, "I match you."

"Never mind," said Harvey, and his voice by habit was severe. But he grinned suddenly and said, "No hurry."

Coffee had thinned the fog of unreality, and Harvey could begin to realize again. Harvey was practical. He went down to the brushwood hut, a little mocking, saying, "Mr. O'Leary, would you like to see our artifacts?"

The slender man rose formally from breakfast, and

his haggard eyes were wary and direct. He said, "Would you mind explaining? You're not thinking of my interest."

"No," admitted Harvey, smiling. "Mine. It occurs to me that it might be well to keep you all where I can see you. Some of you might get discouraged and go off and leave us, and we shouldn't like that."

"It occurs to you," said Colin O'Leary, "a little late. Mr. McDougal has already gone."

Slick Harvey made no exclamation. Instantly he knew he hadn't seen old Red this morning; instantly he grasped the implication. He became aware of distances, of weight, of time. You couldn't make much speed with tons of gold; a man on foot could beat you, and the telegraph would flash, and many men would watch the trails along the borders of five countries. If you had to, you could kill two women and four men to keep them still; but not the armies and police force of five governments.

Men would be watching all the places he could melt the gold, and all the places he could handle it as contraband. No normal smuggling, this; the governments of all the world would spend their forces on a prize like this.

No use to kill these people now. No tons of gold could pay you for the garrote or the noose, or even for the swift, sure death of bullets in your face. The Latins always shot you in the face; and Harvey was no tenderfoot. He'd seen men who got rifle bullets in the face.

Time was the one thing that he had to work with; and he knew it instantly. His smile froze and his eyes glazed, but his voice came instantly, demanding, "When?"

Colin O'Leary answered leisurely, "Last night. Soon after you relieved us of your presence, Mr. Harvey."

Malcolm McDougal, eating breakfast, was aware of Harvey coming swiftly down from the brushwood hut, but he didn't rise. Neither did J. G. Hall. The man of millions had no longer any thought of power, but he had the courage to be still; and so had Joan. She didn't even look at Harvey coming down the hill. Her clear young face was white, her head was bent, her red-brown eyes unseeing on a plate of enameled iron—this daughter of a man of millions. Red had told her to let Malcolm do the talking.

Harvey said, "So Red ran out on you!"

Malcolm was silent for a moment. He said slowly, "Put it that way, Slick. I doubt if you believe it."

"Well, O'Leary says he did!"

"I doubt," said Malcolm, "if O'Leary said it just that way. He told you Red was gone. Red told us to let you know. Thought it might give you something to think about."

Slick Harvey wasted no more time, even to try to find which way Red had gone. Only two ways were possible —west to the Urubamba, north to the Amazon. The westward trail was plain along the valley; he sent Nick and Finney that way, galloping where they could gallop, trotting where they couldn't, killing their horses if they had to. Northward, the chance was harder, but the distance less. Fort Lopez lay that way, and there would be a telegraph.

He said to the man named George, "Don't bother much about trying to pick up a trail. Hit straight for Lopez—that'll be almost due north. And don't come back unless you head him off."

The man named George was not a city man; he knew the jungle. He had heard of Red McDougal in these countries now for many years. Big as he was, old Red McDougal didn't seem so much while you were looking at him; yet the man named George was suddenly uncertain. When you didn't see him, Red McDougal loomed tremendous in the light of his reputation.

"Me?" said George. "All by myself?"

"Oh, no," said Harvey, smiling, biting. "I wouldn't think of sending you to trail one man all by yourself. Al's going with you."

"Me?" said Al, afraid, not of a single man but of the jungle.

"You," said Harvey, smiling, biting. "And you'd better get him. You're the guy that's sure to strangle if he gets away. If Red McDougal doesn't see to it, I will."

Al thought it over, and he said to George, "We'll get him, huh?"

"If you don't drag your feet," said George.

Old Red McDougal, moving quietly, left camp three hours before dawn. He didn't hurry; he would have, with luck, five hours' start, and that was all he wanted. He went up the split of Iscacinga, through the hill of gold, and rounded the valley of the vanished lake. Far off across the mud, in the dim starlight, he could see the dim blur of the ruins, stones against the water, where the treasure of an empire had been buried long ago; but in his knapsack he had corn and beans, dried meat and *chuño*—frozen and dried potatoes. Red McDougal thought of one thing at a time.

Plodding, he reached the spillway where the lake had emptied for four hundred years, went down the empty creek bed, northward, toward the Amazon.

He heard a faint, uneasy stirring in the bush toward the Indian village, and he didn't wait for a wooden spear to question his identity. He spoke into the ancient darkness, in the ancient greeting of the peaceful man:

"Be not untruthful, be not idle, be not a thief."

He heard a human breath catch in the darkness, and a voice, human and not grotesque to Red McDougal, answered in shaking gutturals, "Lord, *ccampas nocca, jinollatac*. Be this the same for you as for myself."

And Red McDougal saw the time to come, and knew that he, a human, might not pass this way again; and he did what he could. He said into the darkness, "Hear me now, my son. Say to all human creatures this, what I have spoken: That the law of old shall be the law no more."

The voice answered, shaking, "Lord, I hear."

Content, old Red McDougal plodded on into the north, into the jungle; and the sun came up over the jungle, and he knew it lighted Iscacinga, miles behind. But Red McDougal long ago had learned the wisdom of the forest, of the silent earth. You needed all your strength for plodding, and you only wasted strength by letting thoughts go darting here and there. Plodding, there was one thing you had to master. Time.

You had to fight it for a while, but presently you earned the peace of jungle creatures, plodding; all your strength was in your body, all your consciousness outside, aware of things that might obstruct or hurt your body. All you had to do was eat and sleep and walk. You let the sun come up, go down, come up, go down; you couldn't stop it.

Being human, you had thoughts; you couldn't help it. Being wise, you drove them on ahead.

But something happened to old Red McDougal that could not have happened to a quadruped. Being a man, he drove his thoughts, and his thoughts drove his body when his body could no longer see. He sprained his ankle. That was something that had never happened to old Red McDougal. For a while he lay in darkness, panting, as unthinking as an animal. He unlaced his boot and pulled it off because it hurt.

Because he was a man, he put it on again, laced it as tightly as he could; hauled out his pocketknife and cut a staff and stumbled on as far as he could before he rested for the night. It would be worse tomorrow. Being human, he consoled himself. The pain diverted his attention from mosquitoes.

Red McDougal was well hardened to mosquitoes. He was grateful for them presently; their stings diverted his attention from his ankle. And the sun came up, went down, came up, went down. He struggled on. His thoughts began to escape from his control. He thought of Malcolm as a little boy. He saw the wide, green, smiling country of the Marañon. He said aloud, "You hear me, kid?" But Malcolm didn't seem to hear. Old Red McDougal was ashamed to know that he was talking to himself.

But he still knew where he was going. Lopez. Lopez ought to be due north from Iscacinga, but he couldn't go straight there. He had to limp along the swelling stream in the jungle. Malcolm was back yonder in the hills. You couldn't buck the jungle with a busted ankle, but the stream would lead you to the Amazon. The Amazon would lead you to Fort Lopez.

And the sun came up, went down. For Joan, for J. G. Hall, who trusted him, he had to reach Fort Lopez. And for Ellen. For O'Leary. And for Malcolm. Red McDougal said, "You bluff him, kid. And keep your temper. If you keep your temper—"

Something struck him in the back. It didn't hurt him much; what hurt was the sound that followed, making him realize that he had failed. He plunged into the bushes and crawled off into the bushes, into the jungle, hiding like an animal. He hid a long time, unaware of time. He had time licked. He saw the sun only as light to see by. Like an animal, he lay entirely still, hearing the crashing of the hunt. Then, dimly, through the bushes, in the sunlight, he could see the man named Al.

XXXIII

THE whip crack of the rifle shot had stilled the forest for a moment, but a bedlam followed—wing beats, bird cries, monkey howls; and Al made so much noise that they wouldn't settle. Al forgot to fear the jungle. It was the mystery, the silence that disturbed him, and there wasn't any silence now. Al crashed into the bush. He knew his man was down. He'd seen McDougal stagger when the bullet hit. He'd seen McDougal limping, even before that. McDougal couldn't run. McDougal didn't have a gun. It ought to be a simple thing to find him, finish him.

The man named George, trying to use his bush-trained ears, protested, "Hey! Go easy there!"

Then Red McDougal knew that there were two of them. His ears followed the movements of the man named George; his eyes watched Al. He didn't feel the drag of time. He didn't feel his throbbing ankle, didn't feel the dull pain in his back. Like any jungle creature, blended with the bush, old Red McDougal lay and hid for life.

Closer and closer came the man named Al, pushing his rifle through the bush.

Old Red McDougal smelled the rifle. Closer and closer; Red McDougal smelled his boots. But Al depended on his eyes alone. Old Red McDougal, lying on his side, could see Al's lashless eyes dart here and there.

He saw Al's eyes decide which way to go, and instantly he knew just what would happen. Al would not step high enough.

Before Al's boot struck his, old Red McDougal had begun to move. He saw Al's eyes flick downward, saw the instant triumph there. He saw Al's mouth begin to grin, to open for a shout of triumph, and he saw the rifle drop. But Red McDougal's staff was already lifting; and before Al really saw him, it was pointing at Al's stomach. And for Joan, for J. G. Hall, for Ellen and her brother—and for Malcolm—Red McDougal rammed the heavy staff into the stomach of the man named Al.

The impact of the staff was soundless; but Al's breath drove out a grunt, the sound of swift paralysis. To Red McDougal, waiting for the man to fall, it sounded deafening. He heard the man named George not fifty feet away. Al's eyes flew open and his mouth flew open, and he doubled forward; and a gaunt hand reached and caught him by the throat.

"What say?" called the man named George.

The bird cries and the monkey howls diminished, and there was no crashing in the bush.

"Hey, Al!"

But Red McDougal's luck was with him yet. Some creature scolded in the bush a hundred yards away. Al's legs had thrashed a little; Red McDougal, with his eyes fixed on a bit of sky beyond the tree tops, threw his own legs over them and forced them to be still. Old Red McDougal, who had no religion, moved his lips on soundless words: "Our Father Who art in heaven—"

"Al!"

No answer. Al was still.

The man named George kept shouting, moving in the bush, but Red McDougal presently forgot him. Time was a tricky thing. The only measure of it was the human heart—the clock inside you; and the clock was slowing, pounding, dragging now. You never felt the drag of time while things were happening. The sun had flipped across the sky. The dark was coming, and old Red McDougal had a thing to do.

He dragged his jackknife from his pocket, whittled the thick end of his staff to a wedge and dug in the timeless mold of the jungle. With his gaunt old hands he scraped at the loosened earth and buried the man named Al. He said aloud in the darkness, "Our Father Who art in heaven." Crawling in the darkness, he cut two short bits of a green sapling, lashing them together with a green and limber twig. On the shorter bit, in darkness, Red McDougal scratched a name.

Illegible, of course, but it didn't matter. Nobody would ever read it. Maybe the man named Al had some religion. Red McDougal set the cross in the loosened mold. But the name that old Red had scratched on the cross was "Charley."

Then he found his staff in the darkness, struggled up and struggled on. He couldn't sleep. Not here. He had a flash light, but he didn't turn it on. Dimly he was afraid the man named George might see it, and he didn't want to kill the man named George. He didn't wonder how. Old McDougal, who had never killed a man, was a little sick.

He had a bullet in his back, but he still knew where he was going. North. He fell and slept, and woke and struggled on. The stream swung westward, but he followed it. He knew he didn't have the strength to buck the jungle. He was grateful for the sun, the eye of the timeless gods. It looked away and you were blind; but if you had a thing to do, you waited, and it came again. It favored men who kept on trying.

Time was nothing to a man who had a thing to do. He tried to eat; it made him sick, but it didn't matter. He could struggle on. He knew where he was going. North.

He saw a river. It was not the Amazon; it was the Ucayali. It ran north. He saw an Indian on the river in a balsa. And he knew what language this one spoke. Old Red McDougal didn't know much Ucayali, but he knew enough to try. He didn't shout "*Bueyúnqui!*" That meant "All of you come here," and this was only one. When you meant "Come, one, two or three," you shouted "*Júi!*"

The Indian came. The Indian stared; but this one had seen white men. Red McDougal knew enough to offer to shake hands, and press a silver *sol*, a dollar, into the Indian's hand. These Indians were not savages. Once they had been the servants of a golden state. The state had housed them, fed them, and they toiled and asked no more. But now they knew. White men would take advantage of docility.

These Indians wouldn't work unless you tricked them into taking money. That obliged them to give value in return. Old Red McDougal tumbled into the balsa. It was merely a long bundle of light, buoyant reeds, and his weight all but sank it. But he had a thing to do.

He told the Indian, "Northward. To the Amazon." He knew enough to say, not "*Búi,*" which meant "Many of us go," but "*Câai,*" which meant "Two of us go."

And then he only knew that he was moving. Northward. Down the river. To the Amazon, the Marañon. The sun was glaring on the river. Red McDougal took his book, the notebook of an engineer, and wrote in the glare of heaven. And the Ucayali flowed without the will of men, flowed northward to the Amazon, the Marañon, the wide, green, smiling country of his dream.

XXXIV

MALCOLM McDOUGAL kept his temper three whole days. At first it wasn't hard. He could still hear his father's rumbling voice: "Just keep your temper, kid. If you can keep your temper—" Red was on his way. Old Red was massive, heavy, slow to make up his mind; but when he started anywhere he got there.

Red would be all right. No man alive could give Red five hours' start and catch him in the jungle.

Harvey came and said to Malcolm, "Shall we come to an understanding?"

Malcolm said, "A good idea."

"Don't kid yourself, McDougal," said Slick Harvey. "I'm not asking you. I'm telling you. If you make just one break, it's going to be too bad."

"For you," said Malcolm. "Think it over, Slick. Suppose you knock us off. What good'll it do you? Red'll have five countries on your trail. Don't think he won't; that's why he went instead of me. They know him; and when he sounds off, they listen. You might get away with murder, but you'd never get away with that much gold.

"Better just fill your saddle bags and beat it while the going's good—you and your boy friend. We won't grudge you all the gold you can carry in your saddle bags. It's worth that to be rid of you."

Colin O'Leary cried, "You can't! They're artifacts!"

"Pipe down," said Malcolm.

"Never mind," said Harvey, smiling with tight lips. . . . "I'm coming to you, O'Leary. You make just one break—one move that we don't like—and we won't bother about you. We'll get your sister. Is that clear?"

"Very," said J. G. Hall. "I suppose that goes for me as well—my daughter?"

"Right," said Harvey. "You're a wise guy, Hall."

"My very close friends," said the man of millions gently, "call me John."

Malcolm McDougal, young and hard and reckless, was aware of things that made him humble. He had never met a situation where you couldn't afford to take a chance. It came to him that there were many kinds of courage. Red had one kind, massive and persistent. This man had another—this tired, aging tenderfoot who kept his dignity when he was helpless.

Malcolm grinned and said, "Okay, Slick. We'll be good. You'll take our word?"

"Hardly," said Harvey. "Mike and I will trust you just as far as we can see you, and no further. Come along. Just watch your step. And never mind that shotgun. I'll take charge of that."

"Okay," said Malcolm.

Joan Hall stared. The sun was sweet on Iscacinga in the morning; Harvey's automatic pointed at Malcolm's stomach, but it didn't seem a deadly gesture. Harvey was smiling. Harvey wouldn't shoot. Harvey was civilized.

The man named Mike said, "Come along."

"Okay," said Malcolm. "Don't get nervous with that trigger, Mike. Observe that we have nothing up our sleeves."

Joan turned away; her lovely, arrogant young face was scornful. Walking beside her up the split of Iscacinga, Malcolm murmured, "Careful, Joan. Don't lose your temper now."

"I won't," said Joan too sweetly, whitely. "If three men must take dictation from one man—two men—what can a woman do?"

"Nothing," said Malcolm. "That's the point. We daren't take a chance."

"I see," said Joan. For there were many kinds of courage, and one kind had nothing to do with common sense. Joan Hall, who lived on fireworks, moved ahead and walked with Colin O'Leary, who could never be expected to furnish any.

Colin wasn't even thinking of the danger. Colin only murmured, "Joan, imagine." He went eagerly into the valley of the ruins; and she saw the still intentness in his eyes, and was aware of things beyond her comprehension. Colin O'Leary drove his sensitive and slender body into hardship constantly—for what? It wasn't gold that stirred him. On his way to gold, with quiet eyes he studied the massive walls of kings long dead.

He climbed on the fallen tower, and he touched the

ancient shapes of gold, battered with stones and slimed with centuries and heaped with modern carelessness; and he was reverent.

The man named Mike said, "Get to work."

"Okay," said Malcolm, and climbed down into the water. And her father followed—J. G. Hall, scrabbling in mud and water under the pistol of a thug!

But Colin didn't even hear. Colin O'Leary was no fighting man, but he was brave.

Ellen O'Leary lingered long enough to whisper, "Joan, don't look so angry. You're too pretty when you're angry," and climbed down into the water like a man. But when she bent to tug at stones, she didn't look exactly like a man. The man named Mike was moved to give her a resounding spank.

Joan stiffened. Nothing happened, though. Malcolm McDougal, grinning—grinning!—merely reached out and ducked the man named Mike in the muddy water. Harvey's gun was out, but Malcolm was still grinning, saying, "Speak to your boy friend, Slick. We can't have that, you know." Mike came up sputtering, but Malcolm's left hand pushed his gun away. Mike couldn't do much, sputtering.

Slick Harvey said, "Behave yourself, Mike."

"Thanks," said Malcolm, and released Mike's gun. It pointed at him, but he grinned, "About that understanding, Slick. We're after gold, not women, huh?"

Slick Harvey had no wish to force the issue. Time was

what he had to fight. Old Red's escape had drawn away four men; and he and Mike were armed, but three men spurred to desperation might have luck—with rocks, with their bare hands. Even the women could put up a fight. Joan Hall, her brown eyes hot, was gripping a slender lamp of gold, not quite as big as a baseball bat.

Slick Harvey snapped at the man named Mike, "Put up that gun!"

Ellen O'Leary gripped no weapon. She had only straightened, facing about; and her gray eyes were steady, watching. When Mike put away his gun she smiled at Harvey, saying "Thanks."

To Harvey. Joan could not believe her eyes.

The sun swung over Iscacinga, and the stones and gold in the water were no longer loose. Malcolm McDougal, engineer, said to Slick Harvey, "Hadn't we better work on the dam? We haven't any diving suits. We'll have to lower the water."

"Maybe you're right," said Harvey. "Anyway, we've got to eat. Knock off for lunch."

As if they were digging ditches for a dollar and a half a day. The gold was heaped about that ring of stones, but there was too much gold. Great tons of junk. Malcolm, whose mind was mathematical, got dizzy when he tried to guess its value. They were all a little crazy, Malcolm knew. He tried to help Slick Harvey comprehend that it was gold. It looked like junk. They knew that it was gold.

Three days the young McDougal kept his red-haired temper. It was all a nightmare; but he had two women on his hands, and Red was gone.

The third day, Nick and Finney came back up the valley from the Urubamba, saying that Red McDougal hadn't gone that way. They said they'd been all the way to the Urubamba. Malcolm knew they lied. You couldn't reach the Urubamba in a day and a half, the way you had to travel on those rocky shelves and through the jungle. Harvey knew they lied; they didn't like the jungle, and they couldn't stay away from gold. Slick Harvey, never loud or violent, took off their skins with words.

Malcolm McDougal didn't hear the words; but he saw the man named Nick, the man named Finney, the man named Mike, and he heard their voices. Harvey's eyes were savage now, and he no longer smiled.

That night in the brushwood hut, Malcolm McDougal masked his fear with flippancy. Joan Hall was flippant too. Colin O'Leary, dazed with the workmanship of hands long dead, could hear the voices from the camp above, and knew that men were animals; and J. G. Hall, the man of millions, had no thought of gold.

Ellen O'Leary washed the dishes. They no longer had two separate camps, except for sleeping; Malcolm, wiping the dishes, heard the voices from Slick Harvey's camp and was on the point of urging Ellen to come down and sleep with Joan, and Colin in the men's tent. Plenty of room, God knew. Three cots were empty. . . . In the camp above the brushwood hut, the man named Mike began to sing. His voice was musical; the song he sang was an ancient love song, strange to hear against the savage loneliness of Iscacinga.

Ellen O'Leary, small and weather-beaten, joined in a soft contralto. Malcolm said grimly. "Stop that."

"Why?" said Ellen, smiling. "I'm just 'singin' in the rain.' "

"You want the rain to come down and sing with you?"

"No," said Ellen; and she smiled, but her lips were trembling.

"Hell!" said Malcolm. "Go ahead and sing. I'm all on edge, but don't you care."

"I know," said Ellen. "Don't you worry, Mac. He'll get there."

"Sure," said Malcolm, patting her cheek. He mustn't make her more afraid.

But she had made him more afraid. He heard the voices, and the tent where he lay that night was lonely. Red was gone, Charley was gone, and there was only J. G. Hall, a tenderfoot. . . . Ellen O'Leary's cheek looked hard, but wasn't. In the night he heard Colin O'Leary's voice.

XXXV

HE COULDN'T hear just what O'Leary said; the brushwood hut was forty yards away. It was the tone that jerked him up on his elbow. J. G. Hall said in the dark, "What is it?"

"Sh!" said Malcolm, listening.

But he heard nothing more. He got up in the dark and said to J. G. Hall, "Stay here." He didn't know just why. He only knew it was up to him. Old Red had left it up to him.

He didn't put on his boots; they would make a noise. He didn't feel the rocks. There was a light in O'Leary's hut, a dimmer light than O'Leary used since they had lent him oil. A flash light. Colin O'Leary had no flash light. Malcolm went up on soundless feet. Through a glassless window he could see the round and blinding eye of the flash light, but its ray was trained below the window. Malcolm kept his temper. He said lightly at the window, "Is this a private party, or—"

The blinding ray jerked up. A gun banged. Malcolm thought he couldn't find the door, but it went with him, backward off its leather hinges, and it struck a man inside the narrow hut. The man was striking at him. With a gun. He grabbed the gun. It banged as he wrenched it loose. The man was Finney. He could see him in the back glow of the flash light on the door. He could smell Finney's breath. He hammered Finney with the gun. Finney was down, but Malcolm whacked his skull again for luck. Somebody else was striking at the man.

Ellen O'Leary. With a book. Malcolm McDougal laughed. But J. G. Hall came through the door, over the broken door, and Joan behind him. In pajamas. Malcolm was a little vexed. He said to Joan, "Get out." Voices were coming down the hill. He picked the flash light up and trained it on the back door of the hut. Slick Harvey came, his pistol in his hand. He wore pajamas, but the man named Mike and the man named Nick were in their underclothes, not very clean.

Malcolm McDougal laughed.

Slick Harvey said, "What's this?"

"You guess," said Malcolm. "Get your trained seal out of here."

Behind the flash light, stooping to lift Finney, he tossed Finney's gun under Ellen's cot. He shoveled Finney into Harvey's arms, but Harvey wouldn't take him. Malcolm let him drop.

He said, "The way I get it, Slick, you're after gold. You may be used to getting away with murder; but don't forget. You haven't got Consolidated Oil behind you now. Red's on his way. You haven't stopped him. If you don't, you're sunk."

Slick Harvey snarled at the man named Nick, "Pick up your buddy and get out."

The man named Finney was reviving, muttering.

Nick helped him up and helped him out. The man named Mike stood staring with some relish. He had never noticed Ellen much, in boots and breeches like a man. The other broad was beautiful, but this one hadn't seemed so much—in boots and breeches.

Malcolm pushed the flash light in his eyes and said, "Go on, Mike. Git!"

Mike got. Then Malcolm swung the light and saw O'Leary on the floor, his head all bloody, Ellen kneeling over him. She wore a torn lacy nightgown. Malcolm had never seen a lacy nightgown. Gals, so far as he knew, wore pajamas. Malcolm was embarrassed. He said fretfully, "Why didn't you sing out?"

"I—couldn't. I know—how a rabbit feels when—"

Ellen's gray eyes quivered, and she toppled on her brother. Malcolm caught her, lifted her and laid her on her cot and tried to arrange the remnant of the nightgown. Bending, he fished under the cot for Finney's gun. His cheek touched Ellen's skin, not weather-beaten.

That was when he lost his temper. He got up and said to Joan, "Look after her," and walked out with the flash light, leaving them in darkness. Harvey and his men had almost reached their camp. Malcolm said, "Wait a minute."

Mike was grinning. Finney was still groggy. Nick, supporting him, was sullen. Harvey was impatient, but he didn't raise his gun. He didn't know that Malcolm had one.

"Stick 'em up," said Malcolm.

Harvey's gun jerked. Malcolm fired. He was no marksman, but the range was short. Slick Harvey yelped and reached for the ancient stars.

The others were already reaching. Malcolm shouted, "Mr. Hall! Bring all the rope that you can find."

"As soon as I can find a match," said J. G. Hall.

Malcolm said, "Take your time. I only hope these birds get tired and drop their hands before you get here."

Harvey staggered and sank slowly to his knees, his hands still up, his eyes half closed; his head sagged and he fell as if he fainted. But his hand fell neatly on the gun that he had dropped. Malcolm McDougal kicked the gun away and said, "Get up. Don't waste it."

Harvey snarled, "You think you're pretty slick!"

Malcolm McDougal said, "That's praise from Cæsar."

He tied Harvey first, jerking the knots tight. Harvey groaned. Malcolm said grimly, "Save it. I wish I'd killed you."

Harvey snarled, "You haven't begun to wish. You'd better do it while you've got a chance."

But Malcolm couldn't, and Slick Harvey knew he couldn't. Malcolm even had to dress Slick Harvey's wound.

The sun swung up on Iscacinga, placidly, as it had swung a thousand million times; but Malcolm was still angry. Colin was still unconscious. Malcolm McDougal cursed the man named Finney. You could stun a man with the flat of a gun; you didn't have to use the edge and break his skull.

Malcolm McDougal said to the man of millions, "Watch 'em. If they wiggle, let 'em have it." He went down to the brushwood hut and said to Joan, "Have you got any films for your camera?"

Joan hadn't. She had used them all while she was still a tourist. Ellen O'Leary, small and weather-beaten, said, "Colin's got films for his."

XXXVI

Ellen was queerly dull. She didn't ask why he wanted pictures; but she got her brother's camera, the tool of an archæologist, too complicated for an amateur. She said, "Maybe I'd better take the pictures for you."

"Sure you're able?"

"I?" said Ellen. "Why, of course. If Joan will stay with Colin. Will you, Joan?"

"Of course," said Joan. "What pictures?"

"Proof," said Malcolm, for his father stood behind him yet.

He went with Ellen into the split of Iscacinga, and they climbed the hill of gold. Malcolm McDougal, engineer, paced measurements, and Ellen snapped the camera at bits of paper—twice at each, a distant shot and then a short one. Ellen's hands were steady, but Malcolm realized how small they were. She was in boots and breeches like a man, but Malcolm was still angry. A hell of a life for a woman—following an archæologist.

Malcolm said roughly, "Sure you feel all right?"

"I'm worried about Colin."

There was no use pretending. Malcolm said, "So'm I," and went on pacing measurements. The best thing he could do was to keep her busy. He said harshly, "Hell! He'll be all right."

"I hope so."

"Sure he will. It isn't in the cards for a man to die just when he—"

"Charley did," said Ellen.

Malcolm was silent, pacing measurements. The sun was sweet on Iscacinga in the morning, and the Andes loomed tremendous, blue, fantastic on the western sky. He tried to say a thing he knew; but Malcolm, like his father, had no gift for words. All he could say was, "Yeah, but he found the gold—the thing he hunted fifty years. And what could he have bought?"

"I know," said Ellen. But the strain had been too much. Her hands were shaking, and her voice was shaking, saying, "Sorry, Mac. I forgot to focus. Will you give me that shot again?"

"Hell, yes!" said Malcolm.

But she sat down on a rock, there on the top of Iscacinga, on the hill of gold, and carefully set down the camera, and wrung her weather-beaten little hands. She said, "I'm sorry, Mac. You'll have to wait a minute."

And he realized how small she was, how delicately made, for all her wiry, weather-beaten look. A wave of tenderness rolled over him. He snarled, "It must be hell to be a woman."

Ellen said, "It is."

"I was afraid of that—last night."

"I don't mean—that. I think I was too scared to realize. And I knew you'd come."

"Did you?" said Malcolm awkwardly. She didn't

answer; only sat there, staring with wide gray eyes into a land not tamed by men. He said. "You've had a hard time, kid, but you've got what it takes."

"I know," said Ellen. "Guts. That's what it takes." And she got up and took the camera and said, "Give me that shot again." He held the paper, and she snapped the camera. She cried, "That's what it always takes! Why can't I have a normal life, like other women?"

Malcolm said, "You will. We're going to get away with this, you mark my word. Colin'll be all right; and he'll be rich enough to hire a dozen secretaries, and famous enough to need 'em. You can live anywhere you want to, any way you want to."

"I don't believe it!"

"Neither do I," said Malcolm, grinning, "but I know it. I'll see to it—me, in person, not a moving picture."

And he caught her sunburned little hands and forced them to be still. He drew her into his arms and held her, camera and all; his tenderness was rage. A woman had a right to comfort.

Ellen whispered, "Mac, you're grand."

He grinned and said, "You're telling me?"

Ellen looked up and smiled. He kissed her gently; he was strangely shaken by the passive, virginal submission of her lips. He let her go. An engineer was just as bad as an archæologist. It wasn't right for a woman to have to be so brave.

They went into the valley of the ruins, and they photographed the pile of gold on the fallen tower; but they left it there. Ellen O'Leary's legs had begun to wabble, and he carried her instead of gold.

On the other side of Iscacinga, Colin O'Leary struggled up in his cot and shouted, "What do you want?"

"Nothing," said Joan Hall.

He struggled, striking at her. It was terrible to have to use her strength. She had to throw her body on him, pleading, "Colin, Colin!"

"Oh," said Colin. "Joan."

"Yes. Joan."

He lay a long time staring at her and she saw the fear and anguish in his eyes. He said, "Is Ellen—"

"Everything's all right. Be quiet, Colin."

"That," said Colin, "is the one thing I can do."

Ellen came in and asked, "How is he?"

"Oh, he's fine," said Joan, and went outside before she wept.

Malcolm and J. G. Hall took turns at watching the prisoners. You couldn't kill them, but you had to watch them every minute.

Ellen O'Leary said, "Let me."

"Not on your life," said Malcolm. "It's no job for a woman."

"Why?" said Joan between her teeth. "Afraid we'll be too tender-hearted?"

"Never mind," said J. G. Hall, and had no thought of the strangeness of it—he, a man of millions, tending men bound hand and foot like savage animals, giving them help they had to have as human beings. More obscene than animals.

The man named Finney whined, "I wouldn't treat a dog like this."

"Neither would I," said J. G. Hall. "Be still, or you may get what you deserve."

On the second morning, though, Colin O'Leary thought he could sit a saddle. Malcolm and Ellen brought the horses, and she filled the saddle bags, but not with gold. With food. They couldn't bother with a pack train. Malcolm set out water for the prisoners, and said to Harvey, "On percentage, one of you is bound to get loose pretty soon, and he can untie the others."

Harvey, half fainting, moaned, "Give us a chance."

"I'm giving you a chance. I'm leaving food and horses. But no guns. Don't try to trail us."

Harvey's eyes came open, and he howled, "I'll get you, if I have to trail you till hell freezes over! And I won't forget!"

"Okay," said Malcolm, and walked out. The sound of horses died away from Iscacinga.

Malcolm McDougal had no skill in tying men. Within an hour, once they were free to work at one another's bonds, the men were loose. They heard a sharp explosion far off down the valley, but they didn't know what it meant.

XXXVII

SLICK HARVEY, raging, thought of Malcolm, but the others thought of gold. They had no guns. Under the law, that gold belonged to the government; if they once left it, they might never get it. They had horses. They had mules; they had O'Leary's mules and the pack train Charley Farr had hired, abandoned now. And they had tons of gold.

They were still packing gold when the man named George came back. The man named George had guns; he had his rifle and his pistol, and Al's rifle too. He told them Al was dead, but so was Red McDougal. They still had a chance to get it all.

Malcolm McDougal took one last precaution. Where the water, running a million years through Iscacinga, bearing gold and grains of quartz, had cut a deep defile into the rock, where the horses had to travel on a narrow shelf cut by the hands of men with tools of stone, he found a crevice in the rock and stuffed it with the last of Charley's dynamite and blew the shelf away. It wouldn't stop Slick Harvey, but it would gain time. Harvey would have to turn his horses on that narrow shelf and find another way. There was another way. Harvey had come another way.

If he couldn't turn his horses, that was worse. The horses would be left to die; and men on foot, in this rough country, could walk horses down—especially horses ridden by two women and a sick man. Any man could do it if he knew the jungle. And George knew the jungle. Malcolm hoped the man named George and the man named Al were still far off, hunting Red's fading trail.

Colin O'Leary couldn't sit his saddle long. They camped by the rushing water, noisy as it had been before its interruption of four centuries, and saw where men had washed the gold four hundred, and four thousand, years ago. Colin O'Leary talked. His anguish wasn't physical. Not all. He talked of five months' work abandoned, priceless things stored in the honeycomb of Iscacinga, holding perhaps the secret he would give his life to learn. Not gold.

He talked disjointedly. Joan said, "Be quiet, Colin."

"Sorry," said Colin, and was quiet; and the unseen condor of the gods drew down the flaming sun.

They had no tents. They didn't have to bother about privacy; the darkness hid them. Night, the black puma, climbed the three steps of the world. Colin O'Leary muttered in his sleep; but Joan put out her hand and touched his face, and he was still.

The second day, he sat his saddle seven hours; the third, he was delirious. The fourth, he managed two. The valley opened and the jungle closed, the hot, low-swinging forest, given to monkeys now four hundred years. Colin O'Leary, who had never come this way, was talkative with fever. When he couldn't ride, they had to wait and let mosquitoes bite them. Life was more than time.

Malcolm McDougal rode in silence, hunting the trail old Red had cut—how long ago? Not long; the jungle hadn't closed it yet. Surely old Red was still alive, still going. Malcolm McDougal rode in silence. He had always taken Red for granted, like the Andes, like the Marañon.

They came to the nameless gorge, the earth crack where a bridge had hung to carry gold—not money, but the grim and senseless beauty of a superstition. Malcolm found the crossing Red had found. He led them up the tilted land, through the thinning bush, and saw the dream blue of the Andes fade and break into dull grays and browns of senseless rock, a senseless welter piled to mock the struggles of such things as men. Old Red had bucked it all his life. For what? Not money. And where was he now? Out in the jungle somewhere.

J. G. Hall said thoughtfully, "I see how Red could spend his life building one railroad."

"Yeah," said Malcolm, "and not build it."

"Now he can. No matter who gets the wrought gold, Mac, that must be the greatest body of ore in the world; and we've got our claims."

"Oh, yeah?" said Malcolm.

"Yes," said the man of millions. "You were smart to

think of photographs. If Harvey does pull up your stakes, those photographs are proof in any court."

"You think so?" said the younger man, sardonic. "I'm afraid you haven't met our politicians."

J. G. Hall, who had met politicians, said, "Leave that to me." Riding away from gold, he could begin to vision it. He said, "The world needs gold."

Malcolm said flippantly, "To worship?"

"No. To work with. In the United States, we use bank checks for money; but no other country does. The world still needs a tangible and measurable thing to use for trade, and the world's business has outgrown the supply of gold."

Malcolm rode savagely into the bush and said, "So what?"

Joan Hall, impatient, rode behind him, and her clear young face was eager now. She saw the world returning, and the thought of it no longer bored her. She said happily, "New York!"

"I've seen New York," said Malcolm.

Ellen O'Leary rode behind with Colin. She was used to that; since she was seventeen, the suns of Arizona and New Mexico and Yucatan had burned her. She had seen New York—from the door of a museum. Ellen O'Leary tried to think of gold, of Colin able to hire proper outfits and a dozen secretaries, Colin famed in his profession; of herself with money to live anywhere she chose, in comfort, normally, like other women.

Riding in boots and breeches, Ellen O'Leary dreamed of pretty clothes.

They came to the edge of the tilted land; Malcolm and Ellen got the horses down to that narrow shelf where, if you fell, only the condors need have interest in you. Horses were not built for going steeply, dangerously down. You had to help them, coax them. Ellen O'Leary, struggling with them, dreamed of a level land.

She rode on a ledge above a bottomless ravine. Ellen O'Leary was afraid of heights, but she was used to them.

That night the forbidden mesa, the last barrier that shut away the world, loomed silent, undefended now. The Urubamba lay beyond, and the traveled trail of Indians. In the morning they went up that awful stair, built for the feet of porters bearing gold. Colin O'Leary saw the crumbling fortress at its head, but had no time to study it. No strength. He clutched the saddle, for the way was open and the horses galloped. Iscacinga faded on the eastern sky, no longer to be distinguished from a thousand peaks; the split had faded. Malcolm and Ellen got the horses down the southern stair, and Colin saw the crumbling temple at its foot. But Malcolm saw the traces of the ancient road, high on the hills, built with tremendous labor long ago—miles shorter than the Indian trail along the Urubamba. It was lost, forgotten, overgrown.

The work of man. It crumbled slowly, but it crumbled; and the very slowness of its dissolution proved the shortness, the futility of effort.

They went down into the valley, into the jungle, to the easy, rambling trail along the stream. You couldn't fall out of the bottom of a valley. And the Urubamba flowed without the will of man, backward and northward to the Ucayali, to the Amazon, the Marañon, the country of old Red McDougal's dream.

Malcolm rode doggedly behind. It was behind them that the crack of a rifle came, and it was Malcolm's horse that stumbled suddenly and fell.

XXXVIII

THE bush was low here; and before he hit the ground, Malcolm had time to know how far that shot had come, to guess that George and Al were back, to wonder what had become of Red. Then he was up and shouting, "Keep your heads down! Beat it! Kick 'em along!" The others all drew rein instead, seeing his horse down. Grinning, waving exasperated hands, he snapped, "Want me to write you a letter? Beat it! And keep going till you hit a village. I'll be with you. Hike!" The bullet must have grazed his hip; it had hit the horse's neck. The horse was stunned. The wound might not be fatal, but the flies would get him. Malcolm snatched his pistol—Finney's pistol—and did what he could.

That harsh explosion jarred them into motion, made them realize that he was armed and competent. Ellen said, "Good luck!" and slashed her quirt across the rump of Colin's horse and spurred her own beside him, watching that Colin didn't fall.

Colin O'Leary shouted, "We can't leave him!"

Ellen said, "He knows better than we do."

Malcolm didn't. But he knew you couldn't bet a hundred-dollar bill against a grain of corn. Two women. . . . Crouching behind a bush, he heard the thud of racing hoofs recede and come. He saw the man named

George come riding fast, his reins loose and his rifle in his hands. He saw the rifle lift. He saw the man's hard, narrow face, his narrow eyes; but Malcolm was no marksman. At a range of twenty feet he shot the horse.

He saw the horse begin to fall. At that speed, Malcolm knew, the man would hit the ground with violence. He couldn't wait to see; Harvey and Mike were close behind, and they had guns. He heard the guns. A rifle and a pistol. Malcolm dived into the bush. He shouted, "Tally-ho, you blankety-blank-blanks!" But he was not facetious. He was thinking of old Red. He wanted them to follow him into the bush. He gripped the pistol, and he crashed with noise into the bush.

He stopped to listen, and he heard the thud of hoofs along the trail. They had refused the bait. Bent double, plunging through the bush, he ran straight at the hill. His memory was trained to register topography. Around this hill, he knew, the Urubamba doubled. Running a mile, he cut off two or three.

But horses on the open trail could easily outrun him. That was why they hadn't followed. They could cut him off and get him after they got the others.

Fighting for breath, he climbed above the bush. They hadn't reached the turn. He saw four heads strung out along the trail—four mounted men. Not George, not Al. He hoped that George was badly hurt. But where was Al?

Topping the hill, he saw the others coming, but not fast. Colin was swaying in the saddle, Ellen trying to hold him. A hell of a life for a woman. . . . Harvey's gang came racing around the turn, and they were gaining fast. Malcolm McDougal's gasping lungs filled suddenly and launched a yell into the sunlit valley:

"This way, Ellen!"

Ellen grabbed at Colin's bridle, wrenched the horses instantly into the bush. Joan and her father followed. Malcolm saw their heads above the bush. So did the distant men. A rifle cracked, and Ellen disappeared. Malcolm McDougal fired insanely, at a range too great for any pistol; and the men came on. The man named George was running at Slick Harvey's stirrup.

Malcolm went leaping down into the bush. But Ellen wasn't hit; they had all dismounted. Malcolm shouted, "Bring the rifles!" Joan ran back, and J. G. Hall ran back. Ellen was helping Colin. Malcolm took Colin's arm over his shoulder and went plowing up the hill. He had already seen where they could make their stand, a cranny in the rocks.

Too late, he realized. It wasn't rifles that they needed. They had pistols. What they needed were canteens. There was no water in that cranny in the rocks.

Bullets began to whistle as they tumbled into it. Two rifles and a pistol; Malcolm began to learn the sound. When one of the rifles cracked the bullet nicked the rock, or you could feel the wind of its swift passing. George was the one to be afraid of.

Harvey's men had disappeared. Peering between the rocks, Malcolm could see a movement in the bush, and fired. He knew he missed. There wasn't anything to shoot at, anyway.

Then George's bullets began to come from a new direction, striking inside the rocks. Where were they coming from? Three hundred yards away, a rocky crag stuck up. Malcolm saw a movement there. Not much to shoot at, but he took a rifle, wedged it between the rocks and tried. He saw the man named George slide down from the crag and run. He fired and missed.

The firing stopped. That was a queer sensation—silence. Malcolm McDougal stiffened all his nerves, but nothing came. Then he could realize.

The rock for fifty yards around their hiding place was bare; and Harvey was no fool. It would be suicide to rush into the open, at close range, in daylight. Harvey would wait for darkness.

XXXIX

A THIN, new crescent moon held back the darkness for a little while. To straining eyes, the rocks about their hiding place were almost luminescent, and the stars were red. Colin O'Leary fought the fever in him, fought to keep his senses all alert, the senses of a jungle animal. But he was not a jungle animal. He was a man. He didn't say he wanted water, for he knew there was no water.

It was he who cried in the darkness after the moon swam down, "Look out!"

Then they were animals. After the instant, icy clutch of fear, they welcomed heat, welcomed the sight of bodies rushing at them in the dark, welcomed the sound of guns to drown the pounding of their hearts. Their own guns blazed; their bodies lay behind the rocks.

The space about them emptied, and they had no sense of time. Minutes or hours might have passed before they heard a hoarse voice pleading, "Water. Water." Then they saw a body lying on the rocks, not far outside the bush.

They had no water, and they feared a trick. Malcolm McDougal yelled into the darkness, "Come and get him! We won't shoot!"

Nobody came. The voice died presently. Colin O'Leary, fighting his need for water, didn't know he gripped Joan's arm.

Joan whispered, "Not so hard."

"Eh?" said the slender man. "Oh! Sorry."

Joan said fiercely in the dark, "Don't be like that!"

"Like what?" said Colin, feverish.

"You go through life apologizing. Don't! Do what you want to, and be damned to anybody that doesn't like it."

Malcolm said flippantly, "You're telling him?"

But none of them knew what he meant. Ellen O'Leary lay in silence and alone. A hell of a life for a woman. . . . Malcolm didn't touch her though. An engineer was just as bad as an archæologist.

The man of millions said, "Be quiet, hadn't we better?"

"Why?" said Malcolm. "Think they don't know where we are? They can wait us out. They know we haven't got any water."

Colin O'Leary groaned. Joan Hall said fiercely, "What's your idea in bringing that up?"

Malcolm said, "I know. My fault. I thought of it too late."

"It's nothing of the sort," said Ellen. "Any of us might have had the sense to think of the canteens."

Joan said, "I naturally supposed—"

"Of course," said Ellen. "You're so used to having other people do your—"

"Stop it," said the man of millions, lying on the rocks, behind the rocks that sheltered him from savage death; and J. G. Hall was wondering why street cars had annoyed him ever. He was sleepy now, and dared not sleep.

The minutes and the hours dragged, and none of them dared sleep. The sun blazed up. Malcolm McDougal watched the lower slope, and watched the trail. Colin O'Leary said in a strange, hoarse voice, "I killed him."

"How do you know?" said Joan.

"That's where I shot," said Colin.

Joan said grimly, "I suppose you're sorry?"

After a moment, grimly, Colin answered, "No."

The man named Finney lay face up, unstirring; and the flies were at him. Malcolm spared him only a glance. He had his own side of the rocks to watch.

The sun swung up, drowsy and hot, but he could still see Harvey's horses in the trail, close to the river. Malcolm wondered just how long it took to die of thirst. He didn't know, and he had more experience of thirst than Colin had, and more endurance. Colin was quite a fellow. . . . Malcolm must have dozed. The firing startled him.

He saw the man named George come running out of the bush, and fired and missed. He cursed his clumsiness and snapped the action of the rifle, but the man was out of range of Malcolm's crevice. Malcolm rose behind his rocks and aimed. The man named George whirled, fired and ran, but there was something queer about it. Malcom tried to aim. Before he fired the man named George threw up his hands and fell.

The air was loud with guns. Ellen was clutching Malcolm from behind. He yelled, "Get down!" Harvey ran past, and Malcolm fired and missed. Harvey had almost topped the ridge before he fell.

Ellen was sobbing, "Mac, we're saved. We're saved."

They were not saved. Bullets were striking all about them, and he dragged her down. He saw the uniforms. The law! Old Red had got there. Grinning, lying behind the rocks, he hugged her, shouting in her ear, "Red got there! He's all right!"

They were not saved. Bullets were whacking, whizzing all about them. Harvey's gang dared not surrender; they had fired against the uniforms. The uniforms came loping through the bush, spraying the universe with bullets. Malcolm waved his handkerchief above the rocks. A bullet snatched it. Then he realized. It wasn't very white. He tore off Ellen's shirt—his own was khaki, brown—and waved it. Men in shabby khaki, barefoot, most of them, went loping past, but spared a glance for Ellen and took time to grin.

Malcolm jammed her back into her shirt and grinned and said, "I'm sorry."

Ellen grinned and said, "Don't be like that!"

Then Malcolm saw a white man coming up the hill. He knew the white man. It was Bill Maycumber, of San Carlos; and the men in khaki were his mine guards—able, in a pinch, to represent the law. Old Red had known the shortest way. Red's will had flashed a thousand miles, the way it had to go by radio and telegraph—across the Andes, down the coast, and back across the Andes to

San Carlos, fifty miles from the Urubamba. Bill Maycumber was a friend of Red's.

Malcolm stood up and grinned and shouted, "Hi, Mr. Maycumber! Am I glad to see you!"

Bill Maycumber trudged in silence up the hill, and his eyes were queer. He gripped the young man's hand. He didn't call the young man Mac, as he had always done. Gravely and awkwardly, Maycumber muttered, "Hi, Red."

XL

Malcolm McDougal rode Slick Harvey's horse, but felt no triumph and not much relief. Not much of anything. The space called time had emptied. On a moonlit evening they rode peacefully into the ranch of Don Cipriano, who had furnished the mules and horses to old Charley; and the world was near. The end of the narrow gauge from Cuzco was around a single loop of the climbing gorge; the distance was the thickness of a single mountain. On the mountain, in the moonlight, they could see the tiny, ghostly walls of Machu Picchu, the dead birthplace of a vanished empire.

Ancient Rubbish Heap!

There was a telephone along the railroad; Don Cipriano had already heard about old Red. Malcolm McDougal stolidly explained about the mules. Their host cried, "I have many horses, many mules, but friends are few such as your father was."

Young Red McDougal bowed impassive thanks. His lean brown face was hard, his blue eyes empty.

But he wasn't hiding grief. He felt no grief. Men died and that was all. Being an animal, he wished to stay alive, but it occurred to him to wonder why. To eat and drink? You didn't need a million bucks for that. A woman? No. A roughneck had no business with a woman. Only women. Work? What could it get you but more bucks? Old Charley had the best of it. He'd seen the gold and died before he had to wonder what to buy.

Old Red was buried at the foot of the Marañon, the country of his dream behind him; but he hadn't lived to see his railroad. Maybe it was just as well. What could a railroad bring to the Marañon but people—swarms of people, jostling, crowding, following a dream; deluded, quarreling and grabbing land—rich farm land, when the world already had more food than it could buy?

Was gold the answer? No. The ones who got it in the end would be the ones who had the most of it already. J. G. Hall, who had more millions now than he could use, talked zestfully of business.

J. G. Hall, sunburned and weatherbeaten, strengthened by contact with the untamed earth, already laid his plans to get the gold.

"Leave it to me," said J. G. Hall.

Malcolm McDougal said without attention, "Sure."

Ellen O'Leary stared at him. He wished she wouldn't. Ellen was small and strange in a woman's dress; her steady, cool gray eyes were queerly big in her small, sunburned face, her shoulders queerly soft and white by contrast with her sunburned neck. It angered him. A woman had a right to comfort. . . . Well, she'd get it now. She'd live in the United States, where she belonged. Her brother could hire secretaries by the dozen.

Colin was sitting on the world. With money, with a man like J. G. Hall to see that he got his share of gold, he could devote himself to archæology—to that queer passion for discovery, for searching in the unknown dark of centuries long dead, not caring that himself and all his dreams must vanish in the dark. Like Red. . . . Well, Colin was a good guy. If his dreams could make him happy, let him have his dreams.

Malcolm McDougal kept the forms; he wasn't strange in tight black velvet breeches and a ruffled shirt, translating stolidly for J. G. Hall.

Joan Hall said gayly, "You can't realize it, can you? It's all over!"

"Yeah," said Malcolm.

Then she saw his eyes, and cried, "I'm sorry, Mac!"

He said, "You needn't be. Red died to win his bet, and I'll bet he was satisfied."

Joan Hall was disconcerted. She could fight with Malcolm, but this hard and cold young man was strange. Colin O'Leary, in the buckskin jacket of a ranchman, wasn't strange; he wouldn't wear it long. The railroad wasn't far away—only the thickness of a mountain.

Colin O'Leary murmured, "Let him alone. He'll be all right."

She said, "You're restful, Colin."

"Ellen doesn't think so," sighed the slender man. "She's game, but it's a hard life for a woman—following an archæologist. And I can't help it, Joan. It's all I know. It's a disease, I guess. I've got to do it—got to go right back to Iscacinga."

"Now?" said Joan.

"As soon as possible. As soon as anybody goes. I can't leave all those things that I've uncovered to be carried off as souvenirs."

"But Ellen needn't go," said Joan. "She can come home with me. An archæologist does get home sometimes, doesn't he?"

"By Jove! That's right," said Colin, and they laughed. "I'm not used to the thought of having money."

"You'll come soon?" said Joan.

Malcolm McDougal saw their laughter finish in companionable silence, and was dully glad. Joan was a game gal too, and she deserved a steady guy like Colin. Needed one. You thought her hair was black, but it was red under its raven sheen—mahogany. A man would have to keep his temper always. Colin could.

Malcolm McDougal couldn't. He was conscious of a dull, slow anger, seeing them dispose of Ellen like a child. But they were right. Ellen O'Leary needed comfort, needed safety. Ellen O'Leary sat there like a child, her gray eyes strange, her little hands hard-clenched, half buried in her woman's lap—the flowing skirts of a ranch woman, her white, tender shoulders very strange. Malcolm McDougal rose abruptly and went out, forgetting to excuse himself.

Forgetting forms. The moon was gone; the hills were

huge and formless, and the starlight had no forms. Men tried to plot the stars in shapes they knew—the Bear, the Cross, the Dipper; but there were no forms. There was no meaning. Men would speak of Red McDougal with respect, now he was gone—old Red, uncertain, massive, fumbling, following a dream into the dark. His son remembered how he used to be, a mighty man, sure of his destiny.

His destiny!

A boy tramped in the purple starlight, and his course was down. You couldn't fall out of the bottom of a valley.

But a girl's voice said uncertainly behind him, "May I come?"

He snarled, "Where to?"

She said, "Wherever you are going."

"Nowhere!"

She said gently, "That's no place to go alone."

He told her savagely, "It's certainly no place to take a woman."

But she didn't answer, only walked beside him; and he heard the Urubamba shouting in the dark—no river, but a wild and turbulent young mountain stream. The hills were wild and formless in the dark.

Then Ellen stumbled, and he caught her arm and swore. He didn't know he bruised her arm. He bent and lifted her long skirts, the many, flowing skirts of a ranch woman, and he saw her high-heeled, silly slippers.

He accused her wildly, "Slippers!"

"Yes. Why not?" said Ellen.

"How well do they fit?"

"Not very."

"Hell!" said Malcolm, and he dragged her to a big flat rock and said between his teeth, "Sit down!"

She sat in silence, and he lit a cigarette and burned it in three savage puffs, tramping and turning in the bottom of the valley.

"You might give me one," said Ellen; and the match-flare burned a picture on his mind—a woman.

"Talk," said Ellen.

"No!" said Malcolm, seeing wide gray eyes and tender shoulders in the darkness. "The one decent thing that I can do is keep my mouth shut."

"You've already kept your mouth shut," said the girl, "too hard, too long. Talk, Malcolm. Get it off your chest."

Nobody but old Red had ever called him Malcolm. Suddenly the dam broke, and the words came—wild and incoherent, bleak and bitter words. Old Red, who gave his life to build a railroad he would never see. Old Charley, who had died the minute he had found the gold. Colin O'Leary, spending his life in hardship, unaware of hardship, seeking things lost and gone into the darkness of eternity. A man of millions, spending all his life in the pursuit of millions he could never use.

He spoke with many words, but all he had to say was, "What's the use?"

The girl was silent while he poured his words into the dark. Then he was empty, and she said, "You liked your father?"

"Huh?" said Malcolm.

"And old Charley?"

"Yes," said Malcolm.

Ellen said, "I don't know what's the use, but I know this: They wouldn't have been the same if they had quit."

"I haven't quit," said Malcolm, but no healing anger rose to give him strength. "I'll build the railroad."

After a moment, huskily, the girl said, "But you won't get anywhere—that way."

"So what?" said Malcolm, shrugging in the dark.

He knew he wasn't going anywhere. He'd always worked, when he could get a job, because he'd always needed money; but he wouldn't need it now. Never again. He'd build the railroad, yes, because old Red had wanted it.

Ellen O'Leary's voice was sharp on the timeless dark: "I think your father was too good a man."

He barked, "You're telling me?"

She snapped, "I'm telling you. I don't believe you've ever thought of it. You're strong and smart and brave, but I don't think you've ever wondered where you stood. You've never had to. You could always just put out your hand and touch your father—in your mind, I mean. He was so big, so real; and now he's gone. You're frightened and don't know it."

But no healing anger rose. His voice was heavy, saying, "Maybe I am. But not because Red's gone. Because I don't see what's the use."

"Maybe there isn't any," said the girl. "Oh, I'm not wise! I only know you—mustn't—mustn't—"

She was silent, and her husky voice had broken queerly, and the starlight queerly glittered on her lifted face—on tears that ran in silence down her lifted face; and rage rose in him then. He had no right to make her feel like that. He wasn't worth it. He was nothing; but he had a handkerchief, a clean one, borrowed from Don Cipriano, and he wiped her face. He didn't mean to touch her face. He knew what it would do to him. It did. He couldn't help it. He sat savagely beside her, held her savagely, but his own face was lifted to the blind, uncaring stars.

He said, "That's right. You go on talkin', kid."

She said against his neck, "I can't. That's all I know."

"You know too much," said Malcolm. "Too damn much. Oh, kid! I've got to kiss you—once."

Ellen O'Leary sobbed, "Just once?"

He snarled, "Just once!" and did it—once, while the Urubamba shouted in the darkness—once, until she struggled and protested, gasping, "Wait, I've got to breathe," and made him realize that she was choking with her tears. He laughed, and Ellen laughed, and then he kissed her—once, till he remembered, and he thrust her off and groaned, "Oh, no, kid, no! I've got to build that railroad!"

"Now?" said Ellen, and the starlight glittered on her cheeks.

He tried to tell her that she needed safety, shelter, comfort—not the wild, great, fertile valley of the Marañon, but the United States, that was already what the Marañon would some day be—lousy with people, cultivated, ordered, tame, a place where people could be comfortable, safc when they were old; but he was young. He cried, "But you're a woman!"

"Oh!" said Ellen. "So you've noticed that!"

He kissed her—once; and he forgot to wonder which he'd rather be—a soft and moneyed bum, or an engineer. The answer wasn't in the stars. It was inside.

They never heard the Urubamba, young and wild, beginning its long, steady march to the unknown sea. A formless cliff was great against the stars, topped by a ruined and deserted city—Machu Picchu, Ancient Rubbish Heap; but they no longer asked why men had built it. No man knew. Men had to build and build against the savage world without; no man knew how, the building was inside. Young Red McDougal saw the taller, wilder bulk of Huayna Picchu, the Young Rubbish Heap, where men had never built; he knew the birthplace of an empire had another name. That was Paccaritampu, House of Dawn.